# Irene in Danger

*An Irene in Chicago Culinary Mystery*

*By Judy Alter*

# Irene in Danger

**by Judy Alter**

Copyright © 2021 by Judy Alter

All rights reserved. The unauthorized reproduction or distribution of this copyrighted work, in whole or part, by any electronic, mechanical, or other means, is illegal and forbidden.

Park Place Press

Fort Worth, TX 76110-1233

ISBN 978-0-9969935-7-9 *(digital)*

ISBN 978-0-9969935-8-6 *(trade paperback)*

Editor: Lourdes Venard, Comma Sense Editing

Cover Art Design: Amy Balamut

Release Date: November 2021

This is a work of fiction. Characters, names, settings, and occurrences are a product of the author's imagination and bear no resemblance to any actual person, living or dead, places or settings, and/or occurrences. Any incidences of resemblance are purely coincidental.

## Mysteries by Judy Alter

### Kelly O'Connell Mysteries

*Skeleton in a Dead Space*

*No Neighborhood for Old Women*

*Danger in a Big Box*

*Danger Comes Home*

*Deception in Strange Places*

*Desperate for Death*

*Contract for Chaos*

*Novella: The Color of Fear*

### Blue Plate Café Mysteries

*Murder at the Blue Plate Café*

*Murder at Tremont House*

*Murder at Peacock Mansion*

*Murder at the Bus Depot*

### Oak Grove Mysteries

*The Perfect Coed*

*Pigface and the Perfect Dog*

### Irene in Chicago Culinary Mysteries

*Saving Irene*

*Irene in Danger*

*For*
*Barbara Bucknell Ashcraft*
*Jean McFadden*
*Judy Wieland Fleener*
*And the memory of*
*Eleanor Lee Stephens*
*Friends of my Hyde Park childhood*

# Contents

Chapter One . . . . . . . . . . . . . . . . . . .9
Chapter Two . . . . . . . . . . . . . . . . . . 16
Chapter Three . . . . . . . . . . . . . . . . . 25
Chapter Four . . . . . . . . . . . . . . . . . . 38
Chapter Five . . . . . . . . . . . . . . . . . . 46
Chapter Six . . . . . . . . . . . . . . . . . . . 51
Chapter Seven . . . . . . . . . . . . . . . . . 62
Chapter Eight . . . . . . . . . . . . . . . . . . 70
Chapter Nine . . . . . . . . . . . . . . . . . . 76
Chapter Ten . . . . . . . . . . . . . . . . . . . 83
Chapter Eleven . . . . . . . . . . . . . . . . . 92
Chapter Twelve . . . . . . . . . . . . . . . . . 97
Chapter Thirteen . . . . . . . . . . . . . . . 107
Chapter Fourteen . . . . . . . . . . . . . . . 115
Chapter Fifteen . . . . . . . . . . . . . . . . 122
Chapter Sixteen . . . . . . . . . . . . . . . . 130
Chapter Seventeen . . . . . . . . . . . . . . 139
Epilogue . . . . . . . . . . . . . . . . . . . . 151
From Irene's French Kitchen . . . . . . . . . . 153
About Judy Alter . . . . . . . . . . . . . . . . 160

# Chapter One

Irene Foxglove was flying across the ocean to ruin my wedding. The wedding was in one week. One short week.

That was my first thought when I read her letter. Dated four weeks earlier, the letter had obviously spent some time lost in the system. So much for international mail!

I read it again, making sure she would really be here tonight. If that letter had been delayed one more day, she'd have been stranded at O'Hare Airport. The thought of pretending to Patrick that the letter hadn't come until tomorrow flickered through my mind, but I dismissed it as unworthy.

But something else from the letter worried me even more. "I shall want to promote my cookbook while I am there. I am bringing two cartons. Please arrange a bookstore signing. Perhaps I could be on your TV show?"

How like Irene to order me to help publicize a cookbook I thought she'd never write. I was a bit curious about it. But as I tried to digest what Irene's arrival would mean, I thought back to our—what would you call it? It was more than a business relationship, though I was her gopher for over a year, and yet it wasn't quite friendship. Irene relied on me, and I was glad to be of help—up to a point. My wedding may have been beyond that point.

When I, a naïve girl from Texas, accepted a job, sight unseen, as the assistant to a TV chef, I suppose I had glorified visions in my mind. But I never expected Irene, almost six foot tall or so it seemed to me at first, haughty, temperamental, with a fake French accent, and always a diva. She wasn't even a very good cook—it didn't take me long to realize that I, with no training, knew more about food than she did, with her precious Cordon Bleu training, which also proved to be fake. Yet, for all her pretension and difficult moods, I became fond of Madame, as she instructed me to call her, and when she was incapacitated, I cobbled together rerun segments to keep her show on the air, and when she and her daughter were in real danger, saving Irene became my mission in life. There was something endearingly helpless about her, as though all that bravado was covering up for the neglected kid from a farm in Minnesota.

The cookbook, however, was another story and did not bring back any fond memories. Before she fled to France, Irene Foxglove had been working, with a whole lot of help from me, on a cookbook tentatively titled *Irene's Favorite Forty and Other Recipes*. The truth, as I saw it, was that Irene didn't want to do the work—she wanted me to do it. The project lagged, though we occasionally corresponded about it in the year she'd been gone. But it was still a rough, very rough, draft in my computer. Apparently not so on Irene's end.

How and where could I arrange a signing on such short notice and with no book to show? Irene's expectations, once again, had no relation to reality.

And why this sudden decision? Even four weeks ago, when the letter was dated, it would have been sudden. Months ago, I'd written her that Patrick and I were to be married, but I'd given her no details, and I certainly hadn't asked for help with the food. In my wildest nightmares, I never dreamed she'd feel she had to be at the wedding. After all, she was settled in France and had her small café to run. Wrong! In her spidery handwriting, she said she knew I would need help with the food, and she knew she must arrive a few days before the wedding. Gabrielle would manage the café. Gabrielle? Her totally spoiled, rude, and unlikable daughter manage a café? That would be a disaster. Too late to tell Irene to turn around and go home.

And help with the food? It was all in order, all arranged. Irene would upset all the careful planning I'd done so that I could have everything just as I wanted and yet not go beyond the budget Patrick and I had established. The cake was ordered, the dinner menu set: butler-passed appetizers of deviled eggs, a specialty of my mom, stuffed mushrooms that Patrick loved, and gougères, the latter a tip of the hat to Irene's tutelage. I still remembered how my arm ached the first day she made me beat the dough—and beat it and beat it. For the seated dinner, I'd chosen a pear and Brie salad and lobster thermidor in puff pastry with haricot vert bundles. On my TV show, *Recipes from My Mom's Kitchen,* I cooked basic American foods; for my wedding, I wanted to go upscale and haute cuisine. Patrick said anything but eggplant.

Patrick and I had agreed on only one cake, and I chose the groom's cake. I'd never yet been to a wedding where I liked the traditional bridal cake. Tasteless and pale compared to the groom's cake. We would have chocolate cake interlaced with layers of mousse. My mom protested, and I thought Irene would likely agree with her.

But I was convinced that the cookbook, not the wedding, was behind this sudden trip back to Chicago. Dropping onto one of the kitchen table chairs, I took a sip of my now-cold coffee and forced myself to read the letter yet again, holding the crinkly blue paper so tightly it was a wonder I didn't tear it. No, it wasn't a bad dream. There it was in Irene's handwriting: "Meet me at 11:45 p.m. Air France #245." No please, no thank you, just an order. So typical. Irene would think nothing of asking us to drive clear across the city late at night, at least a twenty-five-mile drive taking well over an hour on those crowded freeways that I dreaded. Thank heaven Patrick was in my life and would drive me. I smiled at the thought. If Patrick weren't in my life and marrying me in a week, Irene would not be coming from France. Maybe.

Where was he anyway? How long did it take to shower? I'd fixed breakfast and then he'd gone back to his own apartment. He didn't have classes this morning, and he said he'd be right back. I was bursting to tell him our wedding would be ruined.

A few minutes later, Patrick found me still seated at the kitchen table, staring into space. "Henny, what's wrong? You look like you've seen a ghost."

I stood up and put my arms around him, feeling his comfort. "A real live ghost, and she'll be here tonight. We're to pick Irene up at O'Hare at eleven forty-five." I waited for his groan of impatience.

Silly me. Patrick slid out of my embrace, and said, "She's coming all the way from France for our wedding? That's wonderful of her. After all, she's sort of family. Wonder if she'll bring Gabrielle?"

I shuddered at the thought. "Gabrielle is staying behind, supposedly to manage the café, though I doubt she has a clue about that. The thing is, Irene will want to cater the wedding." I seriously thought my tone of voice conveyed the complications that lay ahead. Again, silly me.

"Terrific! That will save us some money, won't it?"

Patrick was so far from understanding Irene, let alone the culinary world. "Patrick," I said, stepping farther away from him, "we can't just tell the Palmer House caterer that we're sorry, but we don't need him. We've booked the room and his time. That means if anyone else wanted the space or his services, he couldn't do it. Besides, Irene will not have a kitchen, let alone equipment. No, the idea is ridiculous, but I'll have to be the one to tell her."

"And that will be hard for you," he said, coming closer and wrapping me in his arms. Patrick always knew how to comfort me.

"There is something more," I said. "She's bringing her cookbook and wants me to arrange a signing. What cookbook? As far as I know, it's still an outline on my computer and hers."

"Maybe she wants to surprise you," he suggested.

"She already did," I muttered. Patrick sometimes didn't see the world the way I did. I tried to make myself pick up his positive attitude, but damn! It was hard.

\* \* \*

That night, we drove across the city in silence. Part of me marveled at the city at night, bright with thousands of lights in windows, streetlights, headlights of cars. Even the occasional traffic lights added to the whirl of color. I wondered what people were doing behind those lit windows—was it a cleaning crew? Someone working late, sleeves rolled up, a McDonald's bag next to the desk. Lovers watching television, their arms entwined. Did they realize I was getting married in a week?

What was I, a girl from suburban Texas, doing slicing through the Chicago night with a man I'd never met a little over a year ago? Sure, I hoped for fame, fortune, and romance when I answered that ad for a chef's assistant for a TV show. But not only did I not expect Irene, I had no idea that Patrick, murder, and mayhem lay in my future. And now marriage. I turned to look at Patrick, in part to reassure myself that he was real. When I reached a light hand out to his arm, he flashed me a smile. He was real, all right, and wonderful.

But what I hoped was the start of a flourishing career in the world of television culinary programming didn't turn out to be what I expected. I thought Irene had studied at Le Cordon Bleu in France and was my entrée to the high-powered world of food television. I knew now that Irene Foxglove did not attend Le Cordon Bleu but the one-year program at Kendall College here in Chicago. The station was local, the show's ratings if not in the basement still on the ground floor. Irene's French airs were based on time spent there in her youth as an au pair. All that shared history did not make me any happier about her arrival. I wondered where she'd stay, worrying that she meant to stay in my apartment.

Patrick brought me back to the present moment. "Henny, can't you find a way to involve Irene, so she can save face? And what will we do about that signing?"

"57th Street Books has cookbooks, but I don't know how receptive they'd be. In fact, I have my doubts. And I haven't seen the cookbook yet, don't know if she used my ideas. If it yells 'self-published, vanity press' at you the minute you pick it up, I won't promote it."

"Hey, change that attitude. Go in there all confident and rave about this French chef. And quit judging the book till you see it."

"And when can I study the book and talk to the chef? I have a taping tomorrow morning, and I suppose I'll have to spend the afternoon with Irene. And I'm not taking her into a bookstore with me. She'd ruin any deal I could make by saying the wrong thing. She has no filter."

"As in diva?" he asked, grinning.

"Yeah. Exactly."

My mind skipped from bookstores to wedding, and I worried again about mixing Irene and the intimate event I had planned. Would she take over? Ours was to be a small wedding. I wanted small but classy. Eight people—Irene would make nine. At least she didn't come in as the unlucky thirteenth. Another way to ruin it, but I wouldn't voice that to Patrick. I was a bit superstitious. We had reserved a hospitality suite at the famed Palmer House Hotel, though the minister would perform the actual ceremony in the grand lobby with its incredibly high frescoed ceilings, its gilt figures standing guard, the wall sconces that provided dim light and most likely were by Tiffany. I admit I was a schoolgirl in love with a dream. That lobby was the grandest place I could imagine.

Through Irene's misadventures, I'd gotten acquainted with Betty Peterman, assistant to the general manager of the hotel. I presented my idea to her, and she immediately went to the general manager, a man named Jim Holcomb. He was intrigued by a wedding in the lobby of the hotel—they hosted weddings all the time but never in the grand lobby. Holcomb thought no one would be inconvenienced or disapproving if we were a small group. And it would be on a Sunday night, not a busy time for the hotel.

"Ray Peterman, our historian, talks to small groups in the lobby all the time. No difference."

I loved Mr. Peterman. He was a true gentleman, probably seventy or better, always dressed in a suit with a white shirt and a bright bow tie. He reigned over a small museum on the hotel's mezzanine, and when he held a treasure in his hands, his eyes glowed with excitement. He had shown me ashtrays and coffee cups, celebrity photographs, autographed, of course, and menus of days gone by. He let me hold a rare silver tea kettle and smiled when I admired a wine goblet. Mr. Peterman had an incredible storehouse of knowledge in his brain, and I'd picked it for the wedding colors—a soft, light brown accented by gold and a touch of scarlet. He also helped me order wedding gifts for the attendees—crystal goblets with our names and the date on one side and an etching of the Palmer House on the other.

Back to the present: "You'll like the gougères—little cheesy bites of airy, puffy pastry. Irene could do those. They're time-consuming."

"Just no eggplant, please," he pleaded. Patrick was no stranger in the kitchen. He was a good cook, but he stuck to things like chili and spaghetti sauce. Some of my choices, like pâté, were beyond him.

"Well, Irene should be pleased I chose lobster thermidor in puff pastry for the entrée. It was cheaper than tenderloin or a carving stand, both of which Claude suggested. And I think she has a recipe for lobster thermidor in the cookbook." I was beginning to see connections. "Irene will not love Claude. He's not French, and he won't fuss all over her. But he'll be polite and call her Madame. I get along with him great." I sat back with a satisfied smile, suddenly seeing at least one thing that might work out. "I'll introduce them right after tomorrow's taping. Claude can distract Irene." I had no idea then just how irrelevant any distractions from me might prove.

"Terrific! I'm glad you're feeling better about Irene's visit. I want to be sure she feels welcome and included."

Patrick was too nice. He didn't feel that nagging doubt that I did. I was still worried about what kind of trouble Irene would get into.

# Chapter Two

O'Hare Airport is eerily quiet at eleven thirty on a Sunday night. The daytime sense of rush and hurry is gone. A few people scattered in seats in the international waiting area either slept or stared into space. The junk food stalls were shuttered with those wire gates they pull down in airports and malls. Patrick and I found ourselves whispering.

The arrivals board showed that Irene's plane would be at least forty-five minutes late. Of course, it would. I saw that as a sign for the visit. We set off in search of almost anything that was open. Our exploration probably took us blocks, but at last we came to an all-night restaurant and found a relatively clean table—no dirty dishes but some crumbs that needed to be wiped. Like many airport restaurants, it had an air of fatigue about it, from the Formica-topped chrome table to the suspect carpet. The lighting was dim, but not dim enough that I missed the stains and crumbs on the floor.

The waitperson who swiped at the table had the same air, her hair coming out of what once had been a ponytail, her dingy yellow apron spotted. Her efforts effectively brushed the crumbs into Patrick's lap. "What'll you have?" Even her voice was flat and tired.

Patrick ordered Coors, and I asked for chardonnay, thinking Patrick was smart to order something in a bottle. I'd check the glass for lingering lipstick stains or fingerprints. Normally, wine late at night would put me to sleep, but this night I was too wired. A glass of wine might calm my nerves, at least I hoped.

Reaching across the now-damp table to hold my hand, Patrick said, "A week from tonight, we'll be a married couple. You know how people always say, 'I can't imagine it?' Well, I can imagine it, and it's wonderful."

I restrained myself from leaping across the table for a kiss. I love it when he gets mushy romantic. Irene would frown. And then I slapped my hand on the table in exasperation. I needed to stop seeing everything as I thought Irene would react to it. She was coming as a guest to a joyful occasion.

Patrick was amused. "Now what's the matter?"

"Nothing," I snapped, the romantic mood broken. "I just remembered something."

"Must have been a humdinger," he muttered. Then, in a soft but firm voice, he said, "Henny, you're building Irene's visit up to be a huge problem. You'll let it overwhelm you—and us. She won't spoil the wedding, but you will if you don't change your attitude."

I squelched the temptation to murmur, "You don't really know Irene." If she didn't directly cause trouble, it was her middle name and followed her wherever she went.

"When are your folks arriving?"

Patrick knew well and good that my family—Mom, Dad, Janie, and Ellie—would be here tomorrow. They were driving from Texas and had planned to stop for the night in Springfield. They were bringing all the fixings for a good, old Texas barbecue, except Dad's smoked briskets, which had been sent ahead and now rested in Patrick's refrigerator. The barbecue would be our rehearsal dinner, held in the rented facility in the pavilion at Promontory Point on Saturday night.

Patrick's parents, who would traditionally host the rehearsal evening, were at first taken aback with my plan, but then I think they were taken aback at me. The wedding was only a week away, and I'd never met my future in-laws. Patrick, bless him, would talk about taking me to Winnetka, where his folks lived, for a weekend. But then something would come up—his father had a golf tournament, his mother was down with a migraine, they were traveling to Europe. My suggestions that he invite them to Hyde Park were met with downcast eyes and "I don't think they're ready for that." Occasionally I'd get little, short handwritten notes, on perfectly proper informal notepaper, from his mother, who wanted me to know how anxious she was to meet me and sorry that it just hadn't worked out. "We all have such busy schedules," she'd say, and I wanted to retort that I could always work time into my days. I never said that.

Of course, I began to build a negative picture in my mind—they were cold fish, maybe they drank too much, maybe they thought they were high society. But then I'd stop and think, "Wait. They produced Patrick and raised him. They can't be all bad." I never did convince myself.

Patrick was the intermediary about the rehearsal dinner and wedding evening. I had to explain to him carefully what brisket and beans meant to Texans, and he was excited about it—to a point. I'd wax enthusiastic, and then I'd sense him drawing back a bit. "It is tradition," he said, "for the groom's parents to host the rehearsal dinner."

"Oh, please, Patrick! Ours is not going to be a traditional marriage, and we won't have a traditional wedding."

"My mother . . ." he began and then his voice trailed off.

I pictured a woman with a blond French twist, a country casual, perfectly tailored pantsuit, and a Burberry scarf thrown casually around her shoulders. And Patrick's father would wear a Ralph Lauren golf shirt—wasn't he a bit old for Lauren?—and atrocious pale green trousers. I had to slap myself back to reality.

One weekend, weeks before the wedding, Patrick disappeared to Winnetka. I was okay with being alone—I could experiment with recipes I'd been thinking about, spend long hours reading, and cry myself to sleep because he'd left me for his parents. I was plainly hurt that I hadn't been invited. The possibility never even came up.

But whatever he said worked, because he reported that the O'Malleys would be glad to host the cocktail hour before the wedding dinner. What Patrick didn't say was that they looked forward to the rehearsal dinner and some Texas barbecue. I could imagine that woman I'd never met asking her son, "Brisket? Who eats brisket? And beans? For heaven's sake, are they barbarians?"

I was replaying all this in my mind, when Patrick interrupted with, "I bet your mom and Irene get along great. They both like to cook. My mom will be the one left out. She prefers restaurants to the kitchen."

I switched to thinking about Mom and Irene and whether or not they'd get along. Patrick gave me a soft punch on the arm and said, "We better head back to the terminal." We made the long trek, but of course Irene's plane was further delayed. It finally arrived at one fifteen in the morning. I wanted to cry out to the gods of airplanes that tomorrow was Monday and I had to be at the studio, bright-eyed and cheery, at nine in the morning. I needed sleep.

Instead of sleep, I got Irene. She was the first one out of the gate. No surprise there. I could imagine her elbowing everyone else out of the way. But if she was first, she must have flown first class. Food for thought.

At five-foot-nine, Irene is always a commanding figure. This night, even more so. Her hair, black when I had last seen her, was now streaked with gray—the kind of silver that most woman would die for—and was pulled back in a chignon, still relatively neat even after the long flight. She wore a blue suit—neither pale nor intense, but a shade in between that I couldn't describe. The jacket was cut boxy and short, held at the neck by what looked to be an antique brooch and parted just enough to reveal a lace blouse underneath. It was sort of a Chanel look a century late. And on Irene, it looked stunning.

She was effusive as she breezed toward us. "What darlings you are to come for me in the middle of the night. I am so thankful." Air kisses on both cheeks for each of us, though she lingered longer at Patrick. Putting her hands on his shoulders, she stared directly into his eyes and said, "You know you're getting a wonderful woman, don't you?"

My strong Patrick never flinched but said, "Yes, ma'am. I do know how lucky I am."

She turned to me, with a long look, and asked, "And you. You will be kind to him, no?"

I really wasn't ready for marriage counseling in the airport, and the way she put her question I wasn't sure if yes or no was the correct answer. I settled on, "Of course," and then changed the subject with, "We must get your luggage."

"Mais, oui! I do not have much, but they would not let me carry it on board. And I do have those cartons of books. I am so anxious for you to see the book, ma chère amie."

I groaned inwardly. I knew what to expect—her luggage would be lost. We stood around the carousel that spits luggage out and waited. Finally, it spit out one or two bags, then a torrent, but none of them Irene's.

"I'll just go ask that nice man at the service desk," she said, sauntering away. Since I'd never had any luck with attendants at luggage carousels, I viewed this skeptically. I could see Irene tilting her head and smiling, and I thought, "Come on, Irene. Coquettish French ways do not work at two in the morning in an American airport."

But the man was on his telephone, and in a minute, two enormous suitcases, the same color of blue as her dress, came crashing out of the mouth of the carousel, followed by two neatly taped cardboard cartons. Irene blew the man a kiss—she actually did—and we left the airport. Patrick loaded her belongings onto a cart and trundled them out to the curb, where she and I waited curbside while he fetched the car. We had little time for all the questions that were burning inside me.

We settled in the car, with Irene in the front passenger's seat because, well, after all, she was the guest. I bit my tongue and crawled into the back seat that I shared with those two enormous suitcases and the books. Just how long did she intend to stay?

Patrick asked the more important question. Where did she intend to stay? I had suffered through daytime nightmares in which she said she'd just stay with us. But when Patrick brightly asked, "Where to?" she answered without hesitation.

"The Palmer House."

I could only hope my gasp of surprise wasn't heard in the front seat. Irene's café in France must really be doing well if she was flying first class and staying at the Palmer House. And she must have totally forgotten that last year when Gabrielle was kidnapped, she had been hidden in the Palmer House. The place should have awful memories for her. While those thoughts tumbled in my mind, Patrick never missed a beat. "The Palmer House it is!" And away we went.

While waiting for the luggage, we'd chatted a bit about French cafes in general. On the ride to the hotel, we got the story of Irene's café. It was in a place called Peyrolles-en-Provence, a farming and wine-making community near Aix-en-Provence.

"Gabrielle is the only café in town. We serve food all day, coffee all day, and wine whenever. So far, is doing good. Is that how you say? People come and they stay—maybe read a book, join a card game, talk with friends. We are the town's meeting place. You order a cup of coffee. Then you stay at table for an hour or more. A glass of wine? We expect you stay longer. What's the American word?"

"Linger?" I suggested. A year in France had made a great dent in Irene's command of English, which was, after all, her native tongue. How much of that was affectation, I wondered, and then silently scolded myself.

"Irene, don't you have to turn tables more quickly than that to make a profit?" This practical question came from Patrick.

"What is this turn tables? We have only ten—plus three on the street outside. But we do not turn them." She paused a minute and then added helpfully, "Some are round." Clearly this chef had never worked in a restaurant.

Patrick explained what he meant, that turning tables had to do with serving new customers frequently enough to make a profit. If she let customers sit for hours occupying one of her few tables, he assumed she could not charge them, and no new paying customer could take the table. She replied only that the café made a small profit. And it was supported by Chance Charpentier, who lived part of the year nearby in Aix-en-Provence.

I gasped again. Chance was the man—villain, if you believed Irene—who was Gabrielle's biological father and, I still firmly believed, the man behind Gabrielle's kidnapping a year ago.

Irene clearly heard my gasp this time. "I introduced them. It was time for Gabrielle to know her father. And he's changed. What do you say? He's aged well." She gave a silly little laugh. "He is a strict father to Gabrielle. That's why I can leave her in charge of café. I know Chance is looking over her shoulder."

I didn't dare ask if the former lovers had decided to let bygones be bygones, and—well, you know. So, I asked what they served that they let people sit all day and still made a profit. "I guess no foie gras," I said, naming the rarest delicacy I could think of.

"Is not allowed by law. No more fattening the poor geese." That silly laugh again, and then she grew serious. "We only offer two or three dishes each day. Maybe a cassoulet or gibelotte and then a lighter dish like Salade Niçoise and maybe an onion and Roquefort tart. Other days we switch—maybe a sole meuniere, or duck confit, or mussels. All depends"—she gave a wave of her hand—"on what I feel like cooking that day." And then, in an undertone, she added, "And what is best in the market."

I thought that a uniquely French approach to food service, and the thought of applying it to my show occupied my thoughts all the way to the Palmer House.

Patrick gave the keys to the smartly uniformed valet, who rushed out to greet us. As soon as Irene's head emerged from the car, the valet said, "Mrs. Foxglove, we are anxiously waiting for you."

Irene gave him a gracious smile, if a bit condescending, and then held out her hand so he could help her stand. Then, with a sharp snap of his fingers, he commanded a bellhop to come retrieve the suitcases and books. I had worried when Irene said the Palmer House that this late at night they might not have a room for her, and an unpleasant vision had arisen in my mind of Madame coming to our side-by-side apartments for the night. But the valet's effusive greeting raised other questions in my mind. It was, put simply, over and beyond for valets who are usually fairly impassive.

At the registration desk, the clerk was equally cordial. "Ah, Mrs. Foxglove, at last. I am so sorry your flight was apparently delayed, but your suite is awaiting you. I will have Benjamin here take you up and get you settled."

A suite, no less. This was getting more and more strange.

All sweet and charming, she turned to us and asked, "Won't you come up?" We both declined on the grounds that it was late—very late—and we had to work in the morning.

"I have a morning taping" I said, "but afterward I could come have lunch with you."

"Delightful! And what are you cooking tomorrow? Can I watch it?"

"Your old favorite," I said. "Sloppy Joe." Even as I said it, I knew it was what Patrick would call my naughty side coming out. I knew Sloppy Joe would irritate Irene. In truth, we were doing a couple of wedding segments this week in honor of my forthcoming marriage.

She drew herself up. "But you must call it Irene's wine casserole."

I tried to look contrite. "Not on a show titled *Recipes from My Mom's Kitchen*. I'm afraid it will remain Sloppy Joe."

"Perhaps I shall have to sue for plagiarism or whatever is appropriate," she said archly, her tone changing in a minute.

My first reaction was that she might really do that. But then I said, "Nope. I've added my own touches. You never did much like the recipe."

Quick as could be, she changed the subject. "I want you to have the first copy of the cookbook. You can have bedtime reading tonight, no?" She motioned to the bellboy and asked him to open a carton. "Please be careful. There are books in there, and we would not want them cut with that box cutter." The bellboy was careful, and Irene extracted a book and handed it to me.

I expected something amateurish. What I held in my hand was first class, an oversize paperback with an attractive cover featuring a truly wonderful picture of Irene in her toque, standing in a kitchen with an AGA range behind her, and pots and pans, obviously well used, hanging above her. I thumbed through quickly—the recipes were neatly laid out, the pages had plenty of white space. It was, in short, well done. I would have to study it closely to see if she had used any of our work, but even a quick glance told me the recipes were French, not the American menu that Irene and I had agreed on. I suspected too that she had found a ghostwriter in France. The cookbook, however, was clearly intended for an American audience and was in English.

"Irene, it's lovely. But you've gone from American to French. There must be a story behind it."

She smiled. "Chance wanted me to publish, but he claimed no one in America cooks French the way I do. He insisted, so what was I to do?" She shrugged, the helpless female subject to the will and wish of a man. Then she added, "He took care of all the details."

And the cost, I assumed. I was astonished, and all I managed to stammer was, "I can't wait until I can find time to sit down and really go through it." I didn't add that there was precious little likelihood that would happen this week.

She changed the subject back to my show. "You must tell me when I can watch the show. And I shall look forward to lunch tomorrow." She gave us each those air kisses again, said, "Bonne nuit," and marched determinedly off toward the elevators, followed by Benjamin and his cart full of luggage.

"Take me home. Please?" I turned to Patrick.

"Yeah," he said. "I'm beat. She sort of sucks the air out around you, doesn't she?"

# Chapter Three

Next morning Patrick dropped me off at the television station and went on to the university for the astronomy classes he taught as a post-doctoral fellow. I was barely on time for my nine o'clock shoot and felt sleepy and out of sorts, but the shoot went well. We were truly doing recipes from my mother's kitchen—the stuffed mushrooms and deviled eggs we would have at the wedding dinner. Mom could make deviled eggs like none I'd ever tasted anywhere but in her kitchen. She might have to help Claude.

When I first told station manager Bob Thorne that Patrick and I planned to marry, he decided to do a wedding-special promotion with the show. In essence, he traded me a week off, for our honeymoon, if I'd let him use the wedding as a promotion. Sounded like a win to me.

"We can do at least two shows," he said, rubbing his forehead, from which the hairline had receded some years ago. He was a big guy, overweight but also with a big frame. What hair he had left was dark and contributed to a five o'clock shadow first thing in the morning. Although he almost always seemed harried and hurried, he was good to work with and had given me a real break by practically inventing a show for me. I was grateful.

Together we planned two shows around the wedding menu—the one on appetizers and another on the barbecue rehearsal dinner, complete with my mom's good beans and appropriate praise for Dad's skill as a pitmaster, an art he'd been perfecting for years. The show would have recipes for potato salad and ranch beans, both from Mom's kitchen, of course. Made my mouth water to anticipate that meal, so familiar from every family holiday all my growing-up years. I was still a Texas girl, even if I lived in Chicago.

That Monday morning Bob teasingly said, "You look a little tired this morning, Henny. Wedding jitters getting to you?"

I managed to avoid yawning in his face as I said, "Irene flew in for the wedding last night."

He rolled his eyes. Having once cancelled Irene's show because he found out she had misled him by telling him she'd studied at Le Cordon Bleu, he knew all about my favorite diva. "She going to complicate things for you?"

"Could just happen," I acknowledged. "She's published that cookbook we were working on. I have a copy in my bag. Want to look?"

He took it and said, "I'll look while you tape. Go!"

When the taping was over, Bob had changed his tune suddenly. "This cookbook is a lot better than I expected. I have a million-dollar idea. If she's back in town, why not have her do a guest appearance? She could promote her cookbook. Is there a recipe that you could put together easily?" Then, with a real burst of enthusiasm, he said, "We can do a blast promotion and air it live."

"Live?" I echoed.

"Sure, it will be more natural. What could she fix?"

"Not barbecue and beans," I shot back, as I tried to process the thought of doing a live show and everything that could go wrong. But then I let my mind go back to her description of what they serve at Gabrielle. "How about a Roquefort and onion tart?"

"People eat that? We need something our audience might cook in their own kitchens. Remember—your mom's kitchen."

"How about lobster thermidor?" I countered, knowing the station would pay for the groceries, including the high-priced lobster. "It's what we're serving at the wedding dinner, and I'm pretty sure it's in the book." My fingers were crossed as I said the latter. I'd have to check the index of recipes as soon as I could.

"Describe it. I don't think I've ever eaten lobster. Is it good?"

How do you begin with a man who's never eaten lobster? I already knew that Bob was in the same kitchen as Patrick—spaghetti sauce and chili. So I described the delicate dish. "Lobster chunks in a rich, creamy sauce with shallots and garlic, egg, a bit of brandy, some spices that won't overwhelm the lobster meat, which is itself rich and a bit sweet. You stuff it back into the shell, top with some Parmesan and breadcrumbs, and broil it. Delicious."

He looked at his paunchy stomach ruefully. "Does sound good. You cook live lobster on the show?"

I had to draw the line in the sand somewhere. "No. Live lobster could be a disaster, and extracting the meat is too complicated for a lot of home cooks. We'll use lobster tails." I didn't add my distaste for the process of boiling live lobsters nor did I mention that the combination of Irene, live lobsters, and boiling water was a recipe for catastrophe.

"Can you get all that together in two days?"

Another chore added to my list. "Yes, but Irene will want to be paid for a guest appearance," I cautioned. "She apparently doesn't need the money, but she'll see it as the principle of the thing." I remembered her sly dig last night about Irene's wine stew and plagiarism.

He shrugged. "Offer her a hundred dollars. But call me as soon as you can and let me know if it's a deal. I'll do a blast promotion for forty-eight hours."

An idea began to form in the back of my mind. Maybe 57th Street Books would be more interested in carrying the book if I told them about the TV show. They'd have time to do a bit of pre-publicity for the show, touting the fact that they were the only Chicago bookstore carrying the book.

With the possibility of once again sharing screen time with Irene—either a lark or a problem—bouncing around in my head and the book signing looking just a bit more feasible, I took an Uber to the Palmer House. As I rode, I opened the cookbook to the index and let out a huge sigh of relief when I saw, "Lobster, thermidor, p. 42." At the Palmer House, I marched up to the main desk, and asked for Mrs. Foxglove.

"Ah, of course. Everyone wants to see Mrs. Foxglove. And who may I tell her is inquiring?" the clerk asked smoothly.

"Henny James."

"Ah, Miss James. Mrs. Foxglove and Mr. Peterman are in the Lockwood awaiting your arrival."

Mr. Peterman! What was Irene up to? I expected her to be pacing in her room, impatiently waiting for me to come buy her lunch. Now I didn't know what to expect, but I should have.

The Lockwood was the hotel's casual dining café. The minute I walked in, the hostess greeted me with what I thought was excessive enthusiasm and without even asking led me to Irene and Mr. Peterman.

They sat in a booth, one of those with high sides that almost guaranteed privacy. I faced the awkward decision of which one to sit next to. I chose Irene, but almost reluctantly. For a brief second, I thought the expression on her face when she looked at me was annoyance, but then she flashed me a huge smile.

"Henny, do meet my new friend, Raymond Peterman. Actually, we met by correspondence some weeks ago. I remembered that Gabrielle's grandfather stayed at the Palmer House when he snuck into town to see her. He talked of Mr. Peterman."

That stopped whatever thought I had. "You knew he came to town? And you didn't let him see Gabrielle, just watch from a distance?"

She shrugged as if it were an insignificant matter. "I was still mad at Chance, and Howard would not have liked it." Irene had an irritating way of dismissing any fact that didn't contribute to the image she wanted to project. A woman who separated an old man from his only grandchild was probably not the Irene she wanted Mr. Peterman to know. Nor did she want to talk about Howard, her late husband, murdered, we thought at the time, by a French thug at Chance's instructions. I was having a hard time straightening all this out, but Irene clearly did not want me to pursue it.

Ray Peterman apparently knew all about Monsieur Charpentier and his granddaughter. At least he didn't ask any questions but just smiled at Irene as though what she said made perfect sense. The hotel historian looked just as I remembered—his suit a bit rumpled, his bow tie askew, his smile open and genuine. He was on his feet before I could stammer out that we had met. "We are acquainted," he said smoothly, "although I think Miss James once used my history tour to pump me for information. Am I right, Miss Henny?"

I hate to be called Miss Henny, even by this man that I liked so much. But I did have the grace to blush. "It was for good purpose, Mr. Peterman," I said. "I was hoping to help Irene."

Now she looked really horrified at me. "Whatever did you do, Henny?" she demanded, drawing herself back in the booth as though to distance herself from me. She was wearing another silk suit today, this one a warm peach color, with a pale pink lace something under it. Her makeup was flawless, complimenting the outfit perfectly. She looked, ah, sophisticated. A wild thought went through my mind: had she brought her toque? Would she wear it when we filmed the show? If we did. Or for the signing? If there was one.

"I was looking for information about Monsieur Charpentier," I said, adding firmly, "If I hadn't, you wouldn't have your café today." And Howard might not be dead, I thought, but I didn't add that.

Since Peterman was smiling, I guess she decided that was her best choice too. "Isn't she clever, this protégé of mine?" Irene simply gushed at him.

"Very," he said drily. After a second, he caught himself. "I was so delighted when Mrs. Foxglove—ah, Irene—wrote that she was coming to stay at the Palmer House. The entire staff has been anticipating her visit. A famous chef, from France, a cookbook author, and a wedding. *Comment merveilleux!*" His French pronunciation was a lot better than mine.

How marvelous, indeed! Or it didn't take much to make him happy.

Curiosity got the best of me. "When did you hear from Irene?" I asked him. Seemed to me the entire hotel had known about her visit, but I didn't.

He leaned back and stared at the ceiling, as though thinking. "I guess it's been about three weeks."

Three weeks. What would I have done differently if I'd had three weeks' notice? I didn't know, but a corner of my mind was angry. I channeled Patrick, who would have told me to chill if he'd been there, and then I managed, "I'm sorry I didn't know until yesterday, Irene. I'd have done a better job of planning your visit."

"I think I have plans," she said, smiling coyly across the table.

Peterman was ever gallant. "I will be more than happy to see that Irene is suitably amused during her visit. I'm sure you will have family to attend to."

"I do, but we will of course want to include Irene in all the wedding plans." Did I really say that out loud, when just twenty-four hours ago I'd been moaning about how she'd ruin the wedding? Now, in an abrupt change of heart, I didn't want her to miss a minute of it. I didn't understand myself, but Patrick would have been proud of me if he'd been there. I wished he were sitting at our table, because I was beginning to feel I needed an ally in camp.

I turned what I hoped was a dazzling smile on my favorite diva. "I have an offer for you. The station manager would like you to do a guest spot on my show. He says we can promote the cookbook." I deliberately didn't mention that it would be live.

She was hooked. "A guest spot? Cook on TV again?" Then she grew petulant. "He cancelled my show. I remember that. No, I don't know that I can forgive him."

An unwelcome roadblock in my plan. "Irene, you wouldn't be working with him. It would be you and me, cooking together again, like old times." I was peddling pretty hard here.

Her smile returned. "Yes, those were good times. What would we cook? Not that Sloppy James or whatever you call it."

Softly I corrected, "Sloppy Joe, and no not that. We're using a wedding theme." I nodded. "We talked about lobster thermidor. I know it's in the cookbook." I did not say it would be tails only. She'd find out when it was too late for her to do anything about it.

She clapped her hands like a schoolgirl. "A perfect choice. So elegant," she said. Then she asked slyly, "He will pay me?"

"A hundred-dollar honorarium." Put out like that, on the table, it sounded pretty low, even to me, but I thought the free publicity more than made up for it. "It will be our last pre-wedding show, bumping one we planned to do about my mom's beans and potato salad."

Again, that horrified look. "Beans? Potato salad? Oh, lobster thermidor will be so much better. Of course, I will do it." Then another shrug. "The pay is not so much, is it?"

I ignored that and brightly tried to change the subject. "Maybe then we could have Salade Niçoise for the bridesmaids' luncheon." Mentally I kicked myself. There was no bridesmaids' luncheon because there were no bridesmaids. With two sisters, I couldn't or wouldn't choose one, and two was an absurdity in a wedding with eight guests.

"I will do it," Irene said grandly. "And I will make the Salade Niçoise for the luncheon."

Great. I'd have to fit that luncheon into our schedule and buy those groceries too. I made a mental note to do a shopping list in the Uber on the way home. Then I realized buying lobster and crab this far ahead was not my best idea. "And I'm hoping to arrange a book signing. Perhaps I can work on that this afternoon. The TV show would promote the signing." There I went, spinning wild ideas in the air. When I should be doing a thousand other things, like a fitting for my wedding dress, I was going to be publicizing Irene's book. I turned to Peterman. "While she's thinking, will you join us for lunch?"

"Lunch?" Irene laughed, that silly laugh again. "We are still on our breakfast coffee. I told you we French can linger all day over coffee—and good conversation." She fixed him with another dazzling smile. I couldn't tell if he saw through her or was drawn into her act, but I felt like a voyeur. Surreptitiously my fingers clutched my cell phone, resisting the urge to press one for Patrick.

To collect myself, I looked away from them briefly and my glance landed on a woman who sat in a booth across the aisle and about two down from us. Her appearance was nondescript—brownish hair caught back in what was supposed, I thought, to be a French twist but had strands flying everywhere, a beige jacket over a beige blouse, glasses, and not much makeup. I noticed her precisely because she was so unnoticeable, except for one thing. She wore a silk scarf, a long one, bold with shades of red, blue, and gold. I was pretty sure it was Hermes and also pretty sure it had cost her a fortune.

But her behavior was strange. She had the large menu propped up in front of her face, as though to hide, but in that moment that I looked at her she peered over the top, staring directly at me. *She's watching us deliberately,* I thought. I could only see her because we were both sitting on the outside edge of our booths. The high dark leather backs to the booths prevented Irene and Ray from either peeking around the edge or standing to get a view, so I didn't mention the woman to them.

"Irene," I said almost brusquely, pulling my attention back to the table, "I also do want you to meet Claude, who will cater the wedding."

She played the innocent. "Who is this Claude? I thought I would cater the wedding."

I took a deep breath. "Since we are using the hotel's facilities, it's only right that we use their caterer. And I didn't know you were coming until yesterday. But now, we have to make up for my lack of planning. I hope you will join my family for dinner tonight."

She waved a hand. "No matter. I'm sure I can be of help to this Claude person. And an invitation for dinner with your family tonight?" She was coy again. "My company is already spoken for this evening."

"If that's a problem," Peterman said, "I would bow out and request Irene's company another night."

I'd have to tell Patrick how fast she moved. "No, I'm sure my family will understand and meet Irene another night." In truth, they were bursting at the seams from curiosity about my diva. This roller coaster was rapidly getting out of my control.

Lunch proceeded. Irene declared she was not hungry, having lingered—she shot me a look as she used the word—over breakfast, Ray Peterman ordered a small salad, and I picked at a chopped salad. Periodically, I checked the nondescript woman, as I'd begun to call her in my mind, and she was still there, still hiding behind the menu, still watching us. My imagination ran away with me. She was from France, sent by Charpentier to watch Irene, or she was from the hotel, charged with making sure Irene's visit went smoothly, though why should they be specially concerned about that? Or she was an international spy . . . *stop that, Henny!* I really wanted another look at that magnificent scarf.

With my attention diverted, conversation at our table was slow. But as I pushed my plate away, I asked, "Irene, would this be a good time for you to meet Claude? He should be finished with lunch prep by now."

Peterman was on his feet. "Let me just go fetch him." And he disappeared toward the kitchen, only to return in a minute leading Claude.

Claude was definitely not your average chef, let alone not French. I'd have given him early fifties as a generous guess at his age. He wore no toque, and his longish black hair was caught up in a net—a toque probably wouldn't have set well on that head. I would love to say he had classic, strong features—but he didn't. Even his smile was small, tentative. I'd worked with him enough to know that real talent lay in those hands and that brain, but he had few social graces. He belonged in the kitchen, not on TV as a chef. It occurred to me belatedly that Irene would walk all over him.

And she did. "You're Claude?" she asked, with a tone of disbelief. And then, before I could head her off, "Are you French trained?"

"No, ma'am. I trained right here in Chicago at the Kendall College." Then, as though applying all over again for a job, he added, "Grew up in Michigan. Small town. Short order cooking at fourteen in the local Dairy Queen. I liked it." He shrugged as though that explained his position as head chef at one of the world's prestigious hotels.

His words should have hit home for Irene, because although she tried hard to hide it, Kendall College was where she too had gained her culinary skills, and she was from small-town Minnesota, not a far cry from Michigan.

"But I've been lucky," Claude went on. "Worked in some of the best kitchens in Chicago." As though he'd been asked to provide a list, he almost chanted, "RPM Italian and RPM Steak, Benny's Chop House, even with Rick Bayless at La Frontera."

"Mexican," Irene sniffed. "Can you do French?"

He twisted the towel he held in nervous hands and asked, "What dishes did you have in mind?"

Ray was watching all this intently, and Irene knew it. "Well, I suppose for the wedding, we don't need an all-French menu. But there will be pâté beforehand, won't there?" You'd have thought it was her wedding, but I kept silent. Although I felt sorry for Claude and the way he was being grilled, I was sort of enjoying the show. Irene at her most imperious—and I wasn't the object for once.

Claude was smoother than she gave him credit for. "If Madame wishes to make it. I will be serving deviled eggs and stuffed mushrooms, and Miss James has also requested gougères. Perhaps Madame would like to make those? For the main course, I will be serving lobster thermidor in puff pastry, Miss James' choice."

In real life, he always addressed me as Henny, and I was a bit taken aback by his formality. I could also tell Irene was tiring of the cat-and-mouse game.

I was afraid Irene would pick up on the puff pastry and want to add it to the TV show, but she breezed right on with her own agenda.

"I shall give Monsieur Peterman a list of ingredients I'll need, and I'll plan to make the pâté the day before the wedding and the gougères that afternoon. They must be fresh and piping hot."

"Yes, Madame. I will be happy to work with you." And with a slight bow, he was gone.

*** 

I Uber'd away from the Palmer House a little after two-thirty, plenty of time to stop at 57th Street Books and then dress so that Patrick and I could meet my family at their motel. No grocery shopping for me this day.

The bookstore was blessedly empty. I didn't want to make my unrehearsed pitch in front of a crowd. I wandered back to the cookbook section and idly surveyed the books on French cooking. There weren't many. By the time a young woman came to ask if she could help me, I pretty much knew what I needed to say.

"Hi. I'm Henny James. Maybe you've caught my TV show, *Recipes from My Mother's Kitchen*."

She looked skeptical. "No, sorry, I haven't."

I shrugged. "It's on a local channel, so I'm not surprised. Here's my card." I thrust it into reluctant hands and went right on. "I'm wondering if you'd carry a cookbook by a French chef, meant to help Americans cook French dishes."

"Well," she said, "there is Julia Child."

Caught! I grinned. "Yes, but this is more affordable, and the recipes are more accessible. I've tried some of Child's, and they are a lot of work." She laughed, and I decided I'd met a fellow cook.

"Do you have a sample?"

"Yes, and I'll be glad to leave it and check back with you. But the thing is, the chef is only here for a week. She flew from France for my wedding next Sunday." I crossed my fingers behind my back as I said only a week. I was increasingly afraid she meant to stay much longer.

Her eyes lit up. "How exciting. Best wishes to you." There was a long pause, while I wondered how to reclaim her attention, but there was no need. "It just so happens we had a cook scheduled for Friday night. A Japanese cook who was going to demonstrate tempura. But he's been called away on a family emergency. Would she take that spot?"

"I can practically guarantee it," I said and asked for details. Five to seven, no refreshments, no advance publicity. "As of now, it looks like Mrs. Foxglove will be on my TV show Wednesday, and the station has promised to promote a book signing if I can arrange it."

She looked even more interested. "We usually have a good crowd of browsers on Fridays, but that might bring in some more people. Can she schmooze?"

I rolled my eyes. "Oh, yeah, she's an expert."

My new friend, whose name I still didn't know, said, "I think we have a deal. Let me get you my card, and we'll check back tomorrow. I do have to talk to my manager about this."

I left the bookstore feeling upbeat and optimistic, the most since I'd gotten Irene's letter.

\* \* \*

Patrick has taught me, sometimes painstakingly, to go the extra mile for others, to bend my sometimes stubborn will to what someone else needs. And that is how and why I ended up carting my family downtown for cocktails on their first night in Chicago. They wanted to meet Irene, and if, as the saying goes, the mountain wouldn't come to them, they'd come to the mountain.

Patrick had made a pot of his famous, at least famous to me, spaghetti sauce. But instead of lounging around our apartments, wearing jeans and sweats, we would leave the sauce in the slow cooker, dress in our finest, and head to the Palmer House for cocktails. It was, Patrick assured me, the right thing to do.

And so there I was, back in the Lockwood, though this time in the bar area. Irene was late, of course, but Ray Peterman greeted us, and I introduced my family: my dad, Gene, that lovable, gentle accountant who always seemed a bit befuddled but never really was; Mom, Cindy, full of energy and as outgoing as Dad was quiet; and my sisters, Janie, a luxury travel consultant, and Ellie, the baby, still in college, still uncertain of who she would become. I introduced them with pride and love. And then Irene swept in.

It did not go well. After I did the introductions all over again, Irene zeroed in on Mom. "You must be glad that Henrietta has learned to cook."

Mom looked startled and managed to reply, "Henny has been cooking since she was about seven."

"*Peut-être.* But I taught her French cooking." Irene was talking through her nose, and French came out sounding like "Fraunch."

Mom never backed down easily. "I taught her Texan," she said with some indignation.

"Of course." The tone was haughty, and Irene turned away abruptly, leaving Mom staring at her in disbelief.

I was indignant, but Patrick stepped in. "Irene, I think Henny's sisters have some questions about France." As he said that he was pulling chairs up so everyone could sit around one of the low cocktail tables. I was praying Janie would have intelligent questions about France and luxury travel. Ray Peterman ordered a round of drinks.

When my family gets together, it is a babble of female voices, with Dad watching benevolently from the sidelines. And so it was this time. Irene couldn't put a damper on it. Only Mom sat in smoldering silence. The girls did have questions, prompted by Ray Peterman, who asked about upscale restaurants in Aix-en-Provence. Janie followed with a question about where tourists could get American food if they wanted it. And, of course, with a second round of drinks, everyone had relaxed.

In a brief moment of silence, the diva turned to Ellie and asked, "Are you going to cook like your sister?" And Ellie replied with a firm, "Never! I want to be an ASL translator." And that set them off because Irene didn't know about American Sign Language. They all talked at once about everything, consumed more wine than they should have, and had a grand time.

Like my dad, Ray Peterman stayed on the fringes, watching, enjoying, but not jumping in. He seemed to sense that this was a moment for Irene. Patrick and I stood back too, his arm around me as he whispered, "See? I told you we'd be glad she came for the wedding. She's giving your family a special memory."

"Yeah. I know Mom will remember it."

Patrick winced.

And then I saw the nondescript lady, seated by herself at a restaurant table, not a booth this time, with a clear view of the cocktail area. Still wearing the Hermes scarf. This time no menu hid the fact that she was watching us intently.

"Patrick? See that lady? She's watching us. And she was watching us at lunch. Something's fishy."

"Henny, she's probably just a guest in the hotel. That she's in the Lockwood when you are is coincidence. And if I were eating dinner alone, I'd be watching this crew too. Give your imagination a rest."

I wished I could.

# Chapter Four

On her second full day back in Chicago, Irene Foxglove was accused of murder. For me, the day began way too early with a frantic call from Irene that sent me tumbling back to the days of our shared TV show.

I was still in bed, still sound asleep, when the phone rang incessantly. Whoever it was would not give up, and it finally occurred to me it could be my parents. The whole family was staying at a Best Western at Forty-Ninth and Lake Shore Drive. I wasn't crazy about either the location or the motel and had argued, rather hard, for the Sophy, a small boutique hotel much closer to my apartment. One look at the Sophy's prices, and Mom had said absolutely not. Then I tried for a one-bedroom apartment in a facility meant for longer stays, but Mom said they didn't need a living room, and they'd be fine with two bedrooms, two beds, and a desk in each room.

But it wasn't Mom on the phone. It was Irene. "Henrietta!" Her voice had the shrill tone that I knew signaled desperation, justified or not.

"Irene," I mumbled. "It's not yet seven in the morning. Whatever is wrong?"

"My purse," she almost shouted. "I have gotten the wrong purse. It looks like mine, but it has nothing of mine in it, nothing! There's a British driver's license for someone named Janis Simmons. But here's the worst—there are these little bags of white powder, and one has split, and the powder is all over the inside of the purse. It's a mess. I simply must have some help." Her voice had moderated, but she was obviously still upset. I didn't think calling maid service was a good idea.

Patrick raised himself on one elbow and asked, "What the heck is going on so early?"

Quickly I explained, dismissing the whole thing by saying, "It must belong to someone who's kinky for talcum powder."

He had been slowly coming awake, but now he threw back the covers, jumped out of bed, and yelled, "Get dressed, Henny. We've got to go save Irene."

My first thought was "Again?" I managed to say into the phone, "Irene, sit tight. Patrick says we'll be there as soon as we can." I hung up, turned to him, and asked, "What do you mean, 'save Irene'? Why are you so frantic?"

"Cocaine," he shouted. "That's what those little bags are. Not talcum powder. Cocaine. I'll bet you money."

Not a bet I was taking. We stumbled over each other, pulling on jeans and T-shirts. I ran a brush through my hair and managed to brush my teeth, but that was it. Before I could grasp reality, we were on the Outer Drive, headed downtown. At the hotel, Patrick threw the keys to the bellman and ran through the doors and the lobby, straight to the elevator.

The bell captain came forward, a skeptical look on his face and the words "May I help you" forming in his mouth. But Patrick said, "We're headed to Mrs. Foxglove's suite. She's expecting us." We did not look like guests who should be in the Palmer House at seven thirty in the morning.

Patrick punched the button for the twentieth floor, and we rode upward in fidgety silence. Irene opened her door immediately, still in her dressing gown. "Thank God you're here," she cried fervently.

Patrick and I had talked about a plan in the car, so I tried to soothe her. "Irene, it's not a big deal. We'll call the desk, ask for Ms. Simmons' room number, and make the switch." I did not, would not, mention cocaine, though out of the corner of my eye I saw Patrick examining the inside of the purse.

"Irene?" I asked. "Could you order coffee for three? Right away?"

I hadn't paid any attention to Irene's handbag either when she arrived or during the day yesterday, but now I saw that it was a satchel style, not shoulder bag. It was the kind I thought old ladies clutched (Irene would be so insulted!) by the handle, fairly deep and commodious. But it was quality—a soft buttery leather in a light shade of tan. Not so distinctive that it wouldn't be easy to mistake it. That, I decided, was what this was—one big mistake, easily fixed.

And then I heard Patrick whistle, a long, low sound, followed by, "Henny, come here!" in a more commanding tone than he usually used with me. As I went to his side, he held out a wallet, open to a French driver's license—and the picture of a woman. There was my nondescript woman, the one who had been watching us, twice, in the Lockwood. I stared. With my limited French I could make out enough to learn that Janis Simmons lived in Paris and was born in 1988.

I believe coincidences can happen, but this stretched my belief to the breaking point. A woman, a woman from France if not French, was very obviously watching us—me, Irene, or both, but I doubted it was Ray Peterman and I thought it was probably Irene—and then she and Irene ended up switching purses. By mistake, or so we presumed.

I snatched the driver's license from Patrick, even as he murmured "fingerprints." Ignoring his caution, I almost thrust it under Irene's nose. "Irene," I demanded, "do you know this woman?"

She backed away a bit, as though to get a good look. She looked intently for a long minute, and then turning away, dismissively, she said, "No. Not at all. Why should I?"

"It's her purse you have. And I saw her watching us in the Lockwood yesterday. So let's figure out how you got hers—and she, presumably, has yours."

Irene looked perfectly blank and innocent. I was going to have to pull this information from her. "Think back to yesterday. When was the last time you went into your purse?"

She thought, and I waited, not patiently. Finally, she said, "I think it was when you left the Lockwood, and Ray and I were going to dinner. I went to the ladies' room to, you know, freshen up."

"Okay, here's the biggie. Was there anyone in the restroom with you?"

She shook her head. "I was surprised it was so empty, but, you know, a weeknight and all." She thought a minute. "I powdered my nose and fixed my lipstick and…yes, then I left my purse on a footstool while I went into one of the stalls."

"You left your purse?" I was incredulous.

"You know, they say that women's purses are unbelievably dirty and germ-infested, mostly because we set them on the floor when we use public commodes." Her tone was righteous, as though she would have me know she'd done the right thing.

I swallowed that one. "So, you left it on the footstool, did your business, and came out. Was it right where you left it?"

She shook her head in the affirmative.

I looked at Patrick, who repeated, "It isn't talcum powder."

Irene was now pacing nervously in a tight circle around the living area of the suite. She made me so nervous I wanted to scream.

"What are you saying?" I looked at Patrick.

"I'm saying there's a good chance it's a plant. That nondescript woman, as you describe her, was watching Irene, waiting for her chance to switch the purses. She did it deliberately."

I wished he hadn't said any of that, so I asked. "But why? Why would she foist drugs off on Irene?"

"Henny, I don't think it's just drugs, as you say. I think it's a fortune in cocaine. Why she did it, I don't know. But we should call the police right away." He pulled out his cell phone, but before he could punch in any numbers, Irene went ballistic. "No," she shouted, "no, you must not. No police. Not ever." Reaching, she tried to grab his phone out of his hand and would have done so if he hadn't quickly put his hands behind his back. Irene drew herself up to her commanding height. "I will not allow it."

"You have no choice, Irene." Patrick was firm. "Someone could kill you for this amount of cocaine." He was still holding the phone behind him.

Just as fast as she had flared, Irene seemed to shrink before our eyes. When she spoke, her voice was low and soft. "That's what I'm afraid of."

"What?" I demanded, not understanding. "You can't be afraid the police will kill you."

She shook her head.

Patrick was calmer and gentler. "Irene, why do you have the idea someone will kill you?"

I had to strain to hear her answer.

"A phone call," she said. "Early this morning. A man. Someone I do not know. He said I will be killed if I go to the police. He gave me instructions about returning the purse."

"What were the instructions?"

She shrugged, but there was no Gaelic nonchalance about it this time. "I do not remember. I was too scared to listen carefully. I hung up and called you."

My vision of our wedding faded further into the background. I wondered how Patrick knew how cocaine was packaged and what its value was. Now was not the time to ask. We had to do something. "Wait, Patrick. Don't call the police. Let me call the desk and ask for Ms. Simmons' room number." I picked up the phone even as I spoke, afraid he would grab it from me.

"They won't give it to you," Patrick predicted.

He was right. The hotel switchboard said, "I'm sorry but we're not allowed to give out that information."

A gentle knock on the door startled all three of us. Patrick peeked through the eyehole and said, "Coffee." We were silent as the waiter wheeled in a table with coffee for three and three Danish. And a sterling silver service, of course.

Irene motioned for me to sign the check, and I did because I noticed the tremor in her hands, which had plagued her when Howard was murdered, was back big time. As soon as the waiter left and the door was safely closed, Irene resumed her pacing. My own hands were none too steady as I poured coffee for all three of us.

"Henny, I don't think you're really hearing me. This stuff is more than valuable enough for someone to kill to get it back."

"Kill?" I echoed. That word again. I wished he'd stopped saying it. Surely Patrick was exaggerating. This was all a mistake that would soon be straightened out. "Irene, go get dressed. We'll have breakfast in the Lockwood, not in your rooms."

Like an obedient child, she turned toward the closet, where a valet had hung her clothes. Patrick, on the other hand, looked at me like I'd gone crazy. As soon as Irene disappeared into the bathroom, I said, "Patrick, there's an off chance this Simmons person will be in the Lockwood, maybe looking for us, and we can exchange purses and forget the whole thing."

"Forget the whole thing?" he repeated. "A fortune in drugs lands in our laps, and you think we can just walk away from it." He came and wrapped his arms around me. "Henny, I want to share a wedding with you, not a funeral."

"Stop! You're scaring me."

"Thank God, because that's what I want to do."

Dimly I heard Irene's cell phone ding once, probably indicating a text. I paid no attention. Being in Patrick's arms was more important.

Irene emerged from the bathroom wearing a silk shirtdress that was buttoned all wrong. Shaky hands and nerves. I had to rebutton about half of it, help her tuck her hair in a bit more neatly, and find her a lipstick in the mess that she'd apparently thrown into a drawer in the bathroom. In a corner of my mind, I realized she had settled in for a fairly lengthy stay, more than the week it would take to get us married. Just what I'd been afraid of, but now that seemed a minor worry.

"My purse?" she asked. "Everything is in it."

Patrick stopped her. "Irene, if you didn't look in your purse last night, how did you open the door to your room?"

That silly nervous laugh was the last thing I expected at this moment. "I remembered I had left it in the room. The card you swipe wasn't in my purse. So we stopped at the front desk, and they gave Raymond a duplicate to let me in."

"Does Ray still have that card?"

"As far as I know. Why?"

"Just wondering."

I was tired of this pointless talk. "Come on, you two. Let's go get some breakfast. I'm hungry."

Just as Irene said, "I couldn't eat a thing," there was a knock on the door, this more forceful and emphatic than the waiter had been. I shoved Patrick to the door. This time instead of peeking through that little hole, he called out, "Yes. Who is it?"

"Police," came the one-word tense answer.

As Patrick opened the door, I held my breath and almost closed my eyes. They had come to arrest Irene for dealing in cocaine. If I had been closer to her, I would have reached out for her hand. But when I finally looked at the door to the suite, there stood Detective Al Schmidt, the man who had cleared Irene's name when her late husband went for an early-morning walk and was found dead on the sidewalk, the man who had rescued Gabrielle from a kidnapper when she was held in this very same hotel. Before I could say anything, he looked at me and exclaimed, "Henny James? I hardly expected to find you here. I'm looking for Irene Foxglove."

"I guess," I managed to say, "when you find Irene, you usually find me." He looked just as he had slightly over a year ago—his head maybe a bit closer to bald, his paunch grown an inch or two. From across the room, I saw the spot on the loosely knotted tie at his neck. Yep, it was "our" Detective Schmidt, and I was relieved to see him.

Schmidt took in Patrick and Irene, both standing like statues, and then introduced the uniformed officer. "This is Officer Linda Rutledge, my new sidekick." She was maybe in her mid-twenties, brown hair pulled back off her face, grim looking, as I guessed she should be in this situation, but with a welcoming face. And she looked like she did a serious workout every day. I breathed a slight sigh of relief. Maybe she'd be good with Irene.

Irene jumped in with both feet. "Do you have my purse?" she demanded in her usual haughty tone. I knew full well Irene considered police officers a subspecies, even Al Schmidt, for whom she ought to be more grateful.

Schmidt took a long, slow look at her and then said, "Yes. It's evidence."

"Evidence of what?"

Now his answer was even more deliberate, and I could tell he was watching each of us but mostly Irene. "Murder."

# Chapter Five

I'm not sure if Irene surprised him or not, but she scared you-know-what out of me by letting out one long scream…and then fainting, falling on the floor in a graceless heap.

Officer Rutledge rushed to her side, felt for her pulse, and turned her so that she was lying on her back. To Patrick, she said, "Get me some bed pillows, please." These she put under Irene's legs.

"Can I get water for her?" I asked.

"Not until she can sit up and drink by herself." She was matter-of-fact to me but kind and gentle handling Irene.

Schmidt, meanwhile, wiped an impatient hand across his forehead and walked over to the table, slumping into a chair. "She do this often?" he asked. Then, "I thought you told me she went to France."

"She's back for our wedding," I explained.

He glanced at Patrick. "Wedding? Congratulations, I guess." Turning to his sidekick, "Rutledge, how long she gonna be out?"

Officer Rutledge could barely hide a slight grin. "I have no idea, sir."

"Don't have all day," he said. "This is a murder investigation."

My voice shook, but I asked the question anyway, "Who was murdered?" I already knew the answer.

"Woman named Janis Simmons. Know her?" He started to pull something out of a folder he held, a picture, I presumed.

I stopped him. "Yes and no," I said. "I guess since you have Irene's purse, you figured Irene has the Simmons' person's bag. We looked in it and saw her ID."

"Swell. You messed the fingerprints up."

"Probably," I replied, "but I saw that woman watching us in the Lockwood twice yesterday—once at lunch, and again when my family had cocktails there last night."

Irene must have heard the word "murder" through her fog because she started to stir and mumble. When she opened her eyes and began to struggle to sit up, Officer Rutledge gently helped her and looked at me and mouthed, "Water. No ice."

I got it from the wet bar in the room, and she helped Irene sip. Predictably Irene asked what happened, and we told her.

"Murder," she said. "That's all I remember. That one word."

Schmidt shifted in his chair and let out an exasperated sigh. "That's good. It's an important word. Tell me what you know about Janis Simmons."

"First, I need to get off the floor," Irene said, struggling as though she could stand without help. With Patrick on one side and Rutledge on the other, she made it to standing, and they walked her to a chair at the table where Schmidt sat.

Leaning across the table toward her and pushing away the half-full coffee cups, he repeated, "What do you know about Janis Simmons?"

Apparently affronted that he would come so close to her personal space, Irene leaned as far back as he did forward. "I know nothing about her except that I have her purse that is filled with this nasty white powder that Patrick says is not talcum powder."

Patrick clasped a hand to his forehead, I gasped, and Schmidt looked around the room, spotting the purse. "Rutledge," he said, nodding toward it. She brought it to him, and he opened it—carefully. And then, in a voice I'm sure was heard throughout the Loop, he exclaimed, "Holy Sweet Pete! There's a fortune in here. And it ain't talcum powder."

Patrick was nodding in agreement.

For a long moment, Schmidt sat clutching the bag and staring off into space. Finally, he turned in his chair and faced Irene. "Mrs. Foxglove, we've got a problem. A big one. This bag is full of cocaine, worth a fortune to someone. So, we have to find out why you have it. And we have to find out who killed Janis Simmons. And to add to that, we have to make sure they don't kill you to get it back. Let's talk. It's in your best interests to tell me everything you know."

Irene looked grim. Her left hand, resting on the table, twitched uncontrollably. But she nodded as though she understood. When asked about first missing the purse, Irene described leaving her bag in the restroom while she used the loo. Schmidt asked the same question Patrick had—how she got into her room that night—and got the same answer. Consistency, I figured, was good.

And then I tuned out because I remembered the ding on her phone. Pretty sure I still knew her passcode, I surreptitiously picked up the phone, held it in my lap, under the table, and checked messages. What I saw sent a chill through me.

The message, probably from a burner phone: "Do not tell the police you have the other purse. Your life depends on it. We will send instructions later."

Way too late to read this! Schmidt was already clutching the purse. I slid the phone back on the table and decided to keep quiet about the message. It was probably the wrong decision.

Schmidt, having gotten everything he could out of Irene, turned to me. "Henny, I suspect you know as much as Mrs. Foxglove, so even though you are not at this point considered a person of interest, as she is, I'm going to ask you to be forthcoming and tell me everything you know."

I nodded, bobbing my head like an obedient puppet.

And so, we talked for maybe fifteen minutes more. I recounted spotting the nondescript woman in the restaurant and again in the cocktail lounge. I even told him about the Hermes scarf.

Somewhere in there, Irene looked at her watch and exclaimed, "I have to make a phone call. Raymond is expecting to take me to lunch." She reached for her phone, once again on the table at her elbow.

"Tell him tomorrow," Schmidt growled. "You're liable to be busy the rest of the day." Then, as though it dawned on him belatedly, "Who's Raymond?"

I watched her face and could tell she was about to snap that it was none of his business. As subtly as I could, I nodded, trying to indicate she should be cooperative. I know Schmidt saw me, but thank goodness, so did she.

"A friend of mine," she said distantly. "He works at the hotel."

Schmidt couldn't resist. "He a busboy?" he asked and then grinned at his own joke. But he gave an impatient sigh, looked at his watch, and said, "Go ahead. Make your call. You got two minutes max."

Irene frowned at him, a look that clearly said she would not be bound by his time limits and left the room. But she was back within two minutes and said nothing about her phone call to Raymond Peterman.

I thought it was time to jump in. "Mr. Peterman is the historian at the hotel. He has that little museum on the mezzanine. He has, ah, been very kind to Irene." I figured he could read between the lines.

Schmidt turned to Officer Rutledge. "Make a note to talk to him. Maybe he knows the Simmons woman or can tell us something."

Patrick sat silent, listening intently, through most of this time. But at one point, his phone dinged. I expected him to check called ID and let it go to voicemail. But he didn't. One look, and he silently got up and walked into the bedroom for privacy. I'm not ordinarily a jealous woman, so that didn't bother me. It was what he said when he came back into the living area that multiplied my anxiety.

Schmidt had just said that he was almost finished with what he needed to know immediately, but he'd need us to come to the station to make a formal statement. No problem. I thought Patrick would drive us. I'd have to call Mom and Dad, but they could take Janie and Ellie and do some museum-hopping. I had even given them a map and a list of places to visit.

Patrick's voice was soft. "Henny?" He moved to the bar area, and I got up to see what he wanted. "That was my mother. I have to go home."

My back stiffened. She was trying to make trouble the week of our wedding. But his next words made me ashamed of my selfish self.

Speaking softly, he said, "My best friend since kindergarten... Jim, you've heard me talk about him... an accident. He was on an early-morning bike ride, and a car plowed into him. They don't think he'll make it... I have to go, have to be there for his parents." He was obviously having a hard time getting the words out.

My world tilted. It wasn't his mother making trouble. It was Patrick being who he is. Everything seemed to rush at me. I would have to face the police station and keep Irene calm and entertain my parents by myself.

Five days until the wedding. I had been so anxious for the day to come. Now, I wanted to push it back. Five days wasn't long enough to solve a murder, break up a drug-dealing operation, and make sure Irene was free. And mourn for Jim.

While all this went through my mind, Patrick was whispering in my ear, "I'll probably stay in Winnetka tonight. You'll be okay?"

I wanted to shout that no, I wouldn't be okay. I'd be terrified and lonely and angry. Out loud I simply said, "Of course. You must go." He was long gone by the time I remembered the text on Irene's phone. Instinct again told me not to tell Schmidt about it. Perhaps they would confiscate her phone.

# Chapter Six

My happy thought that we would not be at police headquarters long proved to be a delusion. I thought Irene would have to sign some papers confirming what she'd testified to, and maybe I'd have to do the same. What I did not expect was more interrogation.

No, we weren't in a concrete block room with a scarred Formica table and four miserable chairs. We were in Schmidt's small office, which was almost as uncomfortable. His desk looked like the "To Be Filed" pile of someone who was administrative assistant to six lawyers—piled high with various stacks of papers. He practically had to clear a path in those stacks so he could see us. Obviously, when alone, he smoked the cigarettes I remembered from my first encounter with him, because the small room, with firmly closed windows despite the pretty day outside, reeked of stale smoke.

Irene and I sat on leatherette side chairs that had probably once been pretty nice but now the upholstery was cracking, the springs were shot—one poked me as I sat—and the cleanliness of the wooden arms was suspect.

He cleared his throat. "Usually, I wouldn't question two persons of interest together, but I figure there's no separating the two of you."

I wasn't sure if that was a bad thing or a good thing, and I was tempted to remind him that I was not a person of interest in Janis Simmons' death or the cache of drugs. He had said that not an hour earlier at the Palmer House. I kept quiet. Patrick would have been proud of me.

Before he could get to serious questioning, or what I considered serious, Schmidt's phone buzzed. He answered with an abrupt, "Schmidt," followed by "Send him in. Oh, and tell him to bring a chair."

In a moment there was a knock on the door, and Schmidt growled, "Come in."

John Wilson, Irene's lawyer, struggled in, clutching a briefcase and dragging a metal folding chair. He set the chair up, deposited the briefcase, and turned to Irene with a good-natured comment that belied his anger, "Irene, it's good to see you, although not under these circumstances. I had no idea that you were in trouble. I should be here for you."

She regarded him coolly. "I am not in trouble. This gentleman"—she nodded imperceptibly at Schmidt—"has a problem. Since I have not done anything wrong, I did not think I needed my lawyer."

Wilson almost clasped his hand to his forehead in a dramatic gesture, but he caught himself and turned to me. "Henny, you should have called me."

I was more honest than Irene. "I know," I said, "but until just now I didn't think of it."

Wilson looked at Schmidt, said in a mock-pitiful voice, "See how quickly they forget?" and then held out his hand. "John Wilson, Mrs. Foxglove's lawyer. We, ah, met a year or so ago."

Schmidt actually rose and took the offered hand. "Yes, I remember. And I think it's a good thing you joined us today. Mrs. Foxglove may well need your expertise."

Now that was a frightening note. I liked John Wilson, always had. He was Howard Foxglove's lawyer, privy, I assumed, to how Howard made his fortune, and when Howard was murdered he inherited the care of Irene. He was, in confidential moments with me, realistic about the difficulties of defending and caretaking a diva, but he did it all with an irrepressible good humor and sometimes a sly wit. Even though he was not a criminal lawyer, I was glad to see him that day, but I couldn't help wondering how he got there. One look at Irene told me. She raised one eyebrow and gave me a sort of half smile. She may have said aloud she didn't need a lawyer, but she was taking no chances.

"I'll just sit here and listen," John said, pulling the chair so that it was a bit behind Irene and me, effectively putting himself in an observer's position. The chair squeaked and groaned, and I thought it must be horribly uncomfortable, but you'd never have known from John's attitude.

Schmidt questioned Irene at length, going over everything she had already told him at the hotel. I know full well that's a standard technique to see if a person's story remains consistent. Irene's story did. But then he branched off, wanting to know about her life in France, how she supported herself and so on. She described the café, Gabrielle, and the meager income from it and then, to my surprise, admitted that she got a monthly allowance from Chance Charpentier, the man who had twenty years ago fathered her daughter, Gabrielle. I knew he supported the café, but the allowance surprised me almost as much as did the fact she would admit it in front of John Wilson, who knew that Howard had already left her a small fortune.

The Chance Charpentier story was getting worse and worse. First, I found out he had published the cookbook—and apparently gotten more cooperation from Irene than I ever had—and now I find out she accepts a monthly allowance from him. Why would she take money that she really didn't need from a former lover that she professed, loudly, to despise? I kept quiet, thinking of what Patrick would tell me.

All Schmidt said was, "Spell his name for me." She did, and he carefully wrote it down. "I suppose I can check on him fairly easily. Aix-en-Provence, you say?"

If Irene was as surprised as I was by Schmidt's flawless pronunciation, she hid it and only said drily, "Look in any French newspaper any day."

He looked at her so long without speaking that I think he was interpreting what she had just said. Then he turned to me. His questions for me were both shorter and less penetrating. He was interested in every detail I could tell him about Janis Simmons, and

I tried my best to dredge up more information. But I had pretty much already told him what I knew.

I asked one question, the question that I didn't want an answer to but at the same time felt I had to know. "How did Ms. Simmons die?"

"Strangled."

Just that one word, and I knew. It was the Hermes scarf. And then I had a new thought. "Irene," I asked, "where did you buy your purse?"

"Ordered it from Neiman Marcus," she said. "Even in France, I sometimes don't find the quality I do at Neiman's, and I kept my account there. Still get their mailings. I liked this bag particularly."

Schmidt was watching me carefully.

"Detective, can you send someone to Neiman's on Michigan and see if they carry that bag? Better yet if they remember a woman buying it in the last few days." It was a long shot, but I figured it might pay off.

He looked at me with new respect. "I'll get someone on it," he said, and picked up his phone to bark some orders that contained the words Neiman's, picture, purse.

When the questioning finally stopped, Schmidt seemed to ignore us. He stared at papers on his desk, scribbled on a legal pad, mumbled into the phone. Irene sat perfectly still in haughty superiority to this foolishness, but I squirmed impatiently. I could feel my phone vibrate, and I was beyond anxious to hear from Patrick. I had managed to call my parents, reassure them that though "something came up," I was safe but would be tied up all day. I think my dad sensed that he did not want to know details, and the last I heard my family was going to spend the day at the Art Institute, including a lunch in their upscale dining space.

Patrick had called five times. Each time, the message was vague. "Not as bad as I thought at first. I'll tell you about it when we talk." The, finally, in the fourth call, "Henny, where are you? I'm starting to worry. And I really need to talk to you." Patrick's voice was low, as though he was whispering, but I knew him well enough to know that it was also the voice of grief.

The fifth call brought relief. "Henny? The doctor says they'll upgrade him to stable, whatever the hell that means. Sounds bad to me, but they think it's an improvement. I'll spend the night with my folks. Jim was conscious, even talked to me, so he knows I'm here for him, and I had a good long visit with his parents. They're holding up pretty well. I know it's hard for them seeing him all broken like that, with all those tubes and needles and monitors, but they're troupers." His voice caught, and he simply said, "Later," and hung up the phone.

I stared at the cell phone in my hand. Why hadn't Patrick mentioned his own parents? And why, if Jim was doing better, hadn't he come home to me? I pushed the latter thought aside as selfishness. In a few days, he would be my husband. I guessed I couldn't begrudge his folks one more visit with him while he was still their son. But deep down inside, a flicker of worry tried to fan itself into a flame.

When Schmidt finally looked up from his papers, he said, "Here's what we're gonna do. Mrs. Foxglove, your belongings even now are being moved out of your suite to a regular hotel room."

She opened her mouth to protest, and I knew she was going to say she paid for a suite, and she wanted it. John Wilson reached over and patted her hand as if to reassure her. I was surprised she didn't withdraw the hand.

"The hotel is anxious to avoid any further bad publicity, and they will comp your room. I'm told it's spacious, well outfitted, and you should be most comfortable." He paused to clear his throat. "What's most important is that it will be easier for my people to protect you in this room. I'm assigning Office Rutledge to you for twenty-four, seven until we figure this out."

Now Irene really did protest. "I can take care of myself, and I don't want a stranger in my room. Besides, whoever these fictitious people are that are so desperate to get that purse back, they haven't asked for it or tried. I think this is all—how you say? —a tempest in a teapot."

Did she forget about the phone call? Now was the moment I should speak up about the text. Something held my tongue back.

Schmidt again stared at her for a long moment, so long that I saw her shift in her chair, and I swear her left hand was jumping again. Finally, he spoke, slowly and distinctly. "I don't think you realize what you're up against. These are almost certainly organized criminals who think nothing of killing. Janis Simmons is a perfect example—I'm assuming at this point she was working for them, a courier if you will, and did something to displease them. Perhaps it was changing purses with you. Who knows? But I will find out. Meantime, your life is in danger, and strangling isn't their only method of punishment. Do I make myself clear?"

Her eyes wide, Irene nodded. I guessed she was convinced, for the time being, but I also knew she could talk herself into another mood rather quickly.

Schmidt went on, as though that interruption hadn't occurred. "I think you'll find Rutledge pleasant and good company. She'll be as unobtrusive as possible. But she will be sleeping on a cot in your room, and during the day she'll be acting as your companion—caretaker, if you'd prefer that word. Your other choice is for me to put you in protective custody here."

"Here?" It was plain she didn't understand.

"In jail," I said.

She looked horrified and said no more, but John couldn't resist chiming in. "It's for the best, Irene. We have to be sure you're safe. Detective, I have an employee who could be available to help if needed. Both Mrs. Foxglove and Henny know Benjamin, and he's had combat experience."

Schmidt cleared his throat and said, "Thanks. At this point, I don't want to go outside the department. I'll keep it in mind." Then he turned to me. "I understand your fiancé is out of town for the night. I don't want you in that apartment. I've made arrangements for you to stay with your sisters in their room at the Best Western."

My mouth opened but nothing came out. How did he know all this about my family? I felt like a child whose naughty behavior had been tattled on to her parents. At least he seemed to know—but didn't say—that Patrick stayed in my apartment these days. I was still a bit shy about admitting that. And the Best Western—how did he know my family was there? But a tiny voice in my head said, *Be grateful*. That tiny voice did not need to remind me, however, that

Patrick did not own a gun, and though I was sure he would defend me to the death, he was not exactly a fighter.

Irene and I both found our voices at the same time. Just as I was saying, "I'll need to go to the apartment," she overrode me with a strident, "I will find a third person at dinner intrusive." Back to having it all her way.

Schmidt stared at her for a moment. "May I ask who you plan to dine with?"

She blushed, the diva of a moment ago replaced by a schoolgirl who looked coyly down at her hands clasped in her lap. "Raymond Peterman."

"I'll tell Rutledge to brush up on her history. I'm sure you'll find her an interesting conversationalist." He turned to me. "I'm assigning an officer to you too. He'll stay with you while you go to the apartment, and he or a relief officer won't be far from your room all night. Now, ladies, if you'll just sign these papers."

"I'll need to read what Mrs. Foxglove is signing first," John said. And he quickly added, "Henny's version too."

Schmidt looked exasperated but he handed the sheaf of papers to John, and the rest of us watched impatiently as he read. It took a good thirty minutes, and at that I think he skimmed.

But then Schmidt's plan kicked into action. The last I saw of Irene, she was grumpy about getting into a car driven by Linda Rutledge, who was trying to be pleasant. "Good luck with that one," I thought.

John Wilson again offered Benjamin's services to take me to the apartment, but his offer was declined, and he left after instructing me to call him for the least little thing. I waited in Schmidt's office for the policeman who would drive me to my apartment and took the opportunity to make the other phone calls that were nagging at me. I wanted to call Patrick, but the lack of privacy in Schmidt's office discouraged me. So, I called Bob at the television station and told him the taping was a bit iffy. I didn't exactly say Irene was a murder suspect but used the same phrase I had earlier when I talked to Dad. "Something unexpected has come up." Bob was not as intuitive as Dad, but then he had a business to run. "I got the time scheduled, Henny, and I got an ad ready to run. Let me know by four today."

I didn't point out to him that it was already four. "I'll get back to you in five," I said, and then I interrupted Schmidt, who alternately messed with papers on his desk and talked on the phone. "Detective, is it all right if Irene tapes a cooking show with me tomorrow and does at book signing at 57th Street Books on Friday?"

From the blank expression on his face, I didn't think he had a clue what I was talking about, so I filled him in on her cookbook.

"Rutledge would be with her?" he asked.

"Of course."

He thought for a long minute. "If she's not in jail, those might be very good things. We could maybe smoke someone out."

Later, I would be sorry he said that, but at that moment I was intent on my plans.

Next, fingers crossed that I was telling the truth, I checked the card of the salesperson from the bookstore and called. "May I speak to Elaine, please?" When she came on the line, I did a quick refresher of who I was and what I was calling about. "The TV show is on," I said, "She'll make lobster thermidor. Something people might cook in their kitchens."

"Well, they have to be better cooks than I am, and have a bigger grocery budget," she said, and I laughed in sympathy. "But, really, that's terrific," Elaine went on. "Our manager likes the idea. I can steal enough from this copy of the book to do a flyer. You know, cover, her picture, a blurb even if I have to make it up."

"Thanks. I'm a bit busy this week"—again, no need to mention that Irene was a murder suspect—"so I'm grateful to you for doing all that. We'll see you about four thirty on Friday, with books in hand. Okay? And I'll call the station right now to confirm their publicity will include the signing."

"Okay. I'm looking forward to it."

Just as I finished calling Bob back to confirm the signing, there was a knock on the door, and a young man came in. He proved to be my protector/chauffeur/whatever, a wet-behind-the-ears officer just out of training named Randy Collins. If I thought I was going to be whisked away in a police car, I was mistaken. His car was an ordinary Chevrolet sedan in a sort of nothing shade of blue. But inside it was state of the art, with a mic, a computer, and an emergency light he could pop on the top if needed.

Once I got talking to Randy in the car, I repented of my harsh analysis. He was a nice guy, eager to please, though I wondered how much protection he'd be if I were threatened. He demonstrated his affability, if not bravery, when I asked if we could stop at Whole Foods. I still had to get the ingredients for Irene's lobster thermidor now that it was probable that we could do the taping. Randy followed me, dutifully pushing the grocery cart as I loaded it with lobster and cream and spice. I thought I saw people looking at me strangely and decided it was because they thought I was a cradle-robbing cougar. Randy really was kind of cute. What I didn't know was that Randy was constantly checking out the shoppers as we went from aisle to aisle.

My family was apparently still at the Art Institute or something because the apartments was empty.

"Randy, I need to call my fiancé. I'll just go in the bedroom. Okay?"

He nodded. "Take your time."

Patrick answered immediately. "Henny, you all right? What's going on?"

I recounted the day's happenings for him and assured him that I was fine, I had a bodyguard, and I'd be spending the night with my sisters. He was relieved, but when I asked, "How's Jim?" he was hesitant.

Finally, he said, "It wasn't as bad as Mom led me to believe. She talked about last rites and all that stuff. He's pretty uncomfortable. In fact, he's in a lot of pain, but I don't think his life is in danger. It was Mom's way of getting me up to Winnetka."

My nasty suspicions had not been completely off track. I tried to be philosophical. "Well, you know, after the wedding, they probably won't get much chance to see you without me, so I can sort of understand."

Now he sounded miserable. "No, Henny, you can't. She says they're not coming to the wedding."

The phone flew out of my hand, and I had to scramble around on the floor to get it. "Patrick, what did you just say?"

"You heard me. They're not coming to the wedding. I never told you this, but she always wanted me to marry Maddie."

"Maddie!" I exploded. "She's your cousin. You can't do that. Your children would be, uh, what's the proper word? Challenged is the best I can think of." My indignation was at the boiling point. I'd met Maddie last year when she enrolled at the university. She was everything I wasn't—beautiful, stylish, and rich. And she grew up in Winnetka. I liked her—just not as a wife for Patrick.

"Calm down, Henny. Maddie and I love each other—like a brother and a sister. She's got a new beau. That's why we haven't seen her. She's busy between her studies and seeing him. She calls me occasionally. Not very often."

I still wasn't calm. "Maybe we should postpone the wedding." What was I saying? I was the one who was counting the days. Well, he was too. But just hours ago I'd been afraid murder would make us change the date, and now I was suggesting we do that because I would have a wicked, selfish mother-in-law. Was I serious? I honestly didn't know.

Patrick's reply this time was quick and firm. "Nope. That's why I'm spending the night. I'm going to talk to them. Henny? I love you. Don't make this any harder for me than it is."

I was contrite. "I love you too, Patrick. I'll see you tomorrow. And tell Jim I'm so glad he's going to be okay."

"I will. Talk to you first thing in the morning," he said and hung up.

I reached for something, anything, and my hand settled on the flashlight by the bed. With all the control I could manage, I threw it across the room, and it hit the far wall with a satisfying thump. I restrained myself from yelling the words that came to my mind—my mom would have been so ashamed. To my relief, the flashlight was plastic and didn't break. But the wall had a good-sized dent, and the paint was cracked.

A gentle knock at the door, and Randy called, "You okay in there?"

I yelled back a "Yes" and then called Dad, told him that the something that had come up was a little more serious than I'd let on, and I'd be spending the night at their motel. His tone was wry when he said, "We know. A Lieutenant Schmidt called us."

I promised to tell all over dinner. We agreed that we would meet at the Best Western. And that's what happened. Predictably, Ellie was instantly smitten with Randy, but I thought that was harmless.

I took my family to the Promontory Restaurant for dinner. Mom was aghast when she looked at the prices but not too aghast to order the lobster hash. Dad had the duck breast confit and in his quiet way raved about it. The girls, being less inclined to culinary adventure, stuck with fried chicken, while I followed Mom's lead. I never turn down lobster.

Over dinner I spilled out the whole story about the nondescript woman, the great purse switch, the murder, and the cocaine, even Irene's infatuation with Ray Peterman. My family were by turns, curious, fascinated, and properly horrified, Dad full of concern for my safety, Mom seeing a lever to get me away from Irene and back to Texas (that was so not happening!), and the girls, who were as overprotected as I had been until I came to Chicago, were simply wide-eyed.

# Chapter Seven

Patrick called while we were at dinner, but he didn't have much to say. A part of me thought he just wanted my reassurance, and I gave it as best I could from a table of six, including Randy, in a crowded restaurant. I asked about Jim, and he said he was doing better and that his mom was staying overnight in his room. "They have a sleeper chair and everything. It'll be fine."

I didn't ask about his parents. What could either of us have said? And that was one story I hadn't told my family yet. If I could avoid it, I would never tell them. I did tell him we were at Promontory, and he whistled. "Pretty classy. Is Irene with you?" I almost giggled when I told him she and Ray had a dinner date, but now they had a chaperone in the person of Officer Linda Rutledge. Then, of course, I had to explain all about Linda Rutledge and Randy, something I guess I'd left out of our earlier conversations.

"This Randy," he asked, "how old is he?"

I studied Randy for a minute and guessed, "Twenty-three."

"You like younger guys?" Patrick was joking, sort of. At twenty-six, the same age as me, he could hardly call Randy much younger. But he was also drawing the conversation out, reluctant to get off the phone and have dinner—and a scene—with his parents.

"Not so much. Listen, Patrick, they're serving our food, and I need to let you go. Know that I'll be thinking about you all evening, and I love you." Ellie rolled her eyes, and I ignored her. "Call me later."

"Okay," he said.

On that hopeful note, we exchanged vows of love and disconnected. I wasn't sure if the wedding was coming closer in my mind or receding. And I was bummed that Patrick's family probably would ruin my wedding by staying away, which would make Patrick miserable. First Irene, now the O'Malleys. I had planned so carefully, but I hadn't counted on human nature, unpredictable as it was.

After dinner, the James family spent the rest of the evening in my parents' room, playing Canasta like old times, and exchanging family stories. But it wasn't quite right. It wasn't really like old times, because there was a layer of tension beneath our laughter. Was it the danger or the wedding that was the elephant in the room? Both, I decided. Randy had excused himself after assuring me he would not be far away, but when the girls and I crossed the hall to our room, I saw no sign of him.

Patrick never did call, which was good and bad. It left me worrying and wondering how his talk with his parents had gone, but I realized that with my sisters sleeping inches from me, I would not have been able to talk about anything that mattered—like his parents. Sleep for me that night was elusive and fitful. I heard every noise in that motel—footsteps in the hall or whispered conversations made me jump with anticipation, even the sound of the icemaker next door sent a wave of alarm through my body. I was sure, of course, that the drug people, whoever they were, were right outside the room and would murder us all when they found out I did not have the purse.

I made myself stay in bed and try to at least doze until seven thirty, but then I gave it up as a bad job, crawled quietly out of bed because Janie and Ellie slept on, and pulled on my jeans and T-shirt. Ugh! The clothes I'd had on last night, and no shower, no shampoo. I felt like something the cat had dragged in, but I grabbed my iPad and snuck out the door, intending to call Patrick first thing.

Randy Collins sat on the bench right outside our door, looking fresh and rested. Sinking down next to him, I asked, "Why do you look like you had a good night's sleep and a shower?"

"Because I did. Did you?"

I was beyond grumpy. "No, I couldn't sleep, and this morning I didn't want to wake my sisters, so I couldn't shower. And I didn't bring a change of clothes—just my toothbrush." I pulled away and looked at him. "If I'd known you weren't out here watching, I'd have really been scared—and sleepless."

He grinned. "Someone else was here. Schmidt sent me home, so I'd be fresh and ready for whatever today brings."

That struck a new note of terror. "What do you expect today to bring?"

He shrugged. "I hope some kind of encounter with the people who killed that Simmons woman."

"You want to run into them? I thought the whole point was to stay clear."

"For you to stay clear, maybe, but if we don't ever make contact, how are we going to find out who did it and arrest them?"

I was beginning to see that we viewed the world differently. "You like this kind of stuff, don't you?"

He shrugged again. "I think so. Don't really know. This is the first big case Schmidt has ever assigned me to. I've pretty much been learning the ropes and being a desk cop."

I said out loud what I shouldn't have. "That doesn't exactly make me feel safe."

"You should. I've been through training. I can do it when the time comes."

I stared at him and wondered. If nothing else, his self-confidence was impressive.

"Schmidt said to tell you that the second purse was purchased Monday at Neiman's on Michigan Avenue. The salesperson remembered because the purse is unusual . . . and expensive. She looked at the picture and was pretty sure the dead woman made the purchase."

My mind raced. This would mean that the woman planned ahead to transfer the drugs to Irene. But last week Irene was still in France. So the woman must have targeted her before she ever got on the plane to come here. But if Irene didn't know Janis Simmons, how did Simmons know to target her? How did she know Irene would be flying to Chicago? I said all this aloud to Randy, who looked startled. Maybe he thought I should leave detecting to him.

"It's a long shot," I said, "but could Detective Schmidt check the passenger manifesto for Irene's flight?"

Randy looked doubtful. "I guess so. I'll call him." He got Schmidt on the line fairly quickly, but I nearly laughed aloud at what he said. "Uh, Detective, Henny—Ms. James—she wants you to check the passenger list for Mrs. Foxglove's flight from France. Seems to think that Simmons woman might have been on the same plane." He quickly added, "I'm not sure what that would prove."

Neither was I, but I thought it was worth a try.

My family wanted to sleep late and linger over breakfast, but I had to get ready for the TV show with Irene. Randy and I headed to my apartment. He made me wait in the car, where I felt horribly vulnerable and thought it would have been safer for me to go with him while he "checked things out." I reminded myself he was new at this, despite all that training he bragged about. After several long minutes, he motioned from the door when he decided it was safe for me to come in.

"Nothing upset," he said. "Nobody's been here."

"You sound disappointed."

"I am. I wanted a chance to be a hero."

This whole thing, I thought, was getting out of hand. Randy lounged on the couch, while I showered and then busied myself in the kitchen making one lobster tail into thermidor so we could whip it out of the oven and then collecting the ingredients for the televised process of making it—lobster, cream, and cheese went into the small ice chest; garlic, shallots, breadcrumbs, and herbs into a brown grocery bag, along with a photocopy of Irene's recipe. I'd occasionally glance at Randy and wish that he were Patrick sitting there.

Patrick! I hadn't called him, and he hadn't called, hadn't left a message. I was immediately sure that meant the worst news: his parents held firm. Now I couldn't call because I was running out of time, Randy was watching me, and I didn't want to be upset when I taped the show with Irene. I was so frantic that I cut my finger on the paring knife while I was trying to dislodge the lobster meat from the shell and yet keep the shell intact. I had to send Randy into my messy bathroom to fetch the Band-Aids. Swell! Doing a TV show with a Band-Aid on my first finger.

I didn't know what I was the most upset about—Patrick not being here, his parents being unreasonable, drug dealers after me (I was sure they were), or the Band-Aid on my finger. And then Patrick called.

"Good news," he said. "My dad took a stand, something he doesn't do often, and they'll be in Hyde Park Friday evening. They'll stay at the Sophy. And I'll be home tonight."

I let out an enormous sigh of relief before I glanced at Randy and realized that Patrick coming home would present all sorts of new problems. But I was overjoyed he was coming back, and I'd deal with the problems as they arose. One did pretty quickly.

"My fiancé is coming home tonight," I told Randy.

He grinned. "Good. I'm happy for you. I'll just stay here on the couch tonight and give you all some privacy."

Whoa! That was not what I had in mind, but a glance at the clock told me I didn't have time to argue the point right then. Around noon I called the hotel to make sure Irene was ready—and couldn't find her.

"I'm sorry," the operator said. "Mrs. Foxglove is not in her room."

"Would you try the Lockwood, please?"

She did and reported that she was not there either. Where could she be? That officer should be with her, so surely she couldn't have gotten in any trouble. Then again, Irene could always find trouble. And now she'd brought it to me. If I couldn't find her and she didn't show up for the show, Bob would murder me. Just after he fired me. I called the studio.

"Where the hell are you?" Bob demanded.

Taken aback, I said, "We're not on till one. I'll be there."

"That's not what I'm talking about. That Foxglove woman is already here, telling us all how to do our jobs. You gotta come rescue us." That gentle bear was enraged.

"As soon as I can," I said. Hurriedly I added my toque and apron to the food I'd prepared. A quick change into tailored pants and a long, white cotton shirt, and I was ready. I rushed poor Randy out the door, and we headed for the TV studio, where we found Linda

Rutledge sitting in the tiny lobby. With an inscrutable look, she nodded toward the closed studio door. I left Randy with Linda, imagining the two of them comparing woes.

Irene was indeed giving directions. As I tried to sneak into the studio, her attention was so focused on the lead cameraman she never even noticed me.

"Now, remember, my right side is my good side, so you want to take it from that angle as much as possible. And never ever focus on my left hand. It has a tremor." She made it sound as though the hand were an independent thing and not part of her.

Bob saw me first and, a trifle too loudly, said, "Here's Henny. We can get this show on the road." Under his breath, he muttered, "Literally."

I began setting up the ingredients I'd brought, getting out dishes, etc. Fortunately, there would be little cooking this time, and no pots and pans. Just as I almost had everything ready, my cell phone rang. Afraid that my family was lost in the wilds of Chicago or had met some catastrophe, I said, "One second" to Bob and walked away. But it wasn't my dad. It was Detective Schmidt.

"We ran Janis Simmons' fingerprints. Got a big surprise. They match a French woman named Simone Guillaume"—he carefully spelled the last name for me—"and guess where she lives."

I could feel Bob's impatience and knew I didn't have time for guessing games. "Where?"

"French records list Aix-en-Provence as her home."

I should have guessed after all. "So what does all this mean?"

Long sigh. "It means I have to see if Janis Simmons is still alive. I have my doubts."

Such a strong chill went through me that I shuddered. "Keep me posted," was the best I could manage. "I'm at the studio, about to tape with Irene. Gotta run." But my mind was already racing about the dead woman's identity—why did the picture look like Janis Simmons if the woman I really saw was Simone whatever Schmidt said her name was.

"Okay, Henny, but just know that in my mind this ups the danger to both you and Irene."

*Great! My parents thought I brought them here for my wedding, but in reality, they may be here for my death. I'd ask the identity questions later.*

"Henny, think we could have your attention over here?" Bob's voice dripped with sarcasm, and he was drumming his fingers on a countertop.

"Sorry," I murmured and rushed to stand by Irene. I'd just have to go through the shoot without checking my makeup or hair. Best I could do was kind of tug at the shirt I wore and hope the apron would hide any wrinkles. I smoothed my hair and clapped the toque on my head.

Irene had a dramatic moment when she realized there were no lobster, only tails. "Where are the live lobster? You cannot cook only the tail. It's barbaric." I assured her this was a practical substitution for the home cook who did not have her skills. She nodded sagely, and after that the shoot went well. Irene did drop one of the wooden spoons on the floor when she was starting to stir the sauce. She leaned to pick it up, which would have looked awkward on camera. I nudged her with my elbow, and she straightened right up to smile brightly at the camera. She also forgot all she'd taught me about not fiddling with your hair and holding your hands still when they were not occupied with cooking. Nervous gestures look awful on television. Still, we got through one shoot, and Bob yelled, "That's a wrap."

Irene was angry. "That's all? I thought it was a run-through, so I could get the feel of things again. After all, it's been over a year since I've been on camera."

"No one will be able to tell," I said soothingly. "You did just fine."

Bob simply rolled his eyes. As we left, he half-heartedly wished me a happy wedding, and I told him I'd see him in a week.

It was barely two o'clock, and I figured I could catch up with my family, wherever they were. Of course, Randy would go with me, and maybe Patrick could meet us. I had it all worked out in my mind, but Irene had other plans.

"We will all go for tea at the hotel," she announced grandly.

I knew they served high tea, but I also knew it was not offered until four o'clock. "It won't be ready for another two hours," I reminded her.

"They will prepare it for us." She seemed quite sure of her importance at the hotel. "Mr. Peterman will join us."

We went to tea at the Palmer House.

# Chapter Eight

We had to split up, of course. Randy drove me, while Officer Rutledge escorted Irene. I had two dilemmas on my mind: I couldn't very well call my family and ask them to join us, since Irene was the hostess. And yet, they had come all this way to be with me, and they were seeing darn little of me. I solved that by calling Dad and apologizing that Irene needed me for an hour or two.

"But the good news," I said, "is that Jim, Patrick's friend, is showing some improvement, and Patrick is coming home tonight." A little stretch of the truth there.

Dad asked if that meant the girls would stay at my apartment for a girls-only pajama party long in the planning. That idea, which I'd once encouraged with visions of wine and cheese and gossipy talk, didn't seem so appealing now. And, of course, there was Randy. That gave me my excuse.

"I think the girls should stay at the motel, Dad. I'll ask the lieutenant if he plans to have security there for you, just in case." I was getting pretty good at stretching the truth. I didn't say this aloud to Dad, but I knew Patrick would not be thrilled about Randy's continued presence, let alone my sisters.

And that brought me to my second dilemma: should I tell Irene about the woman named Simone? Perhaps she even knew her. It turned out I needn't have worried. Linda Rutledge had already told Irene.

As we seated ourselves on couches in the grand lobby of the Palmer House, Irene was not in a mood to talk about soaring ceilings and gilt figures. "This is unacceptable," she said as though making a pronouncement. "I will not be a prisoner of fear. I intend to enjoy my return to Chicago."

Somehow out of that the words "return to" caught in my brain. Was she coming back to stay? Leaving Gabrielle in France? Had this all been a great ploy to get rid of Gabrielle?

Linda saw my puzzlement and explained, "I told Mrs. Foxglove about the increased possibility of danger. She, ah, is not taking it well." Irene glared at her, but Linda pushed on. "She says she does not know Simone Guillaume."

"Never heard of her. Aix-en-Provence is a big city. And I am not there often these days. I cannot possibly know everyone. All of this fuss has nothing to do with me. The owner of the purse is dead, or I would give the purse back to her."

I was losing patience with my favorite diva. "It's not that simple, Irene. The purse does not matter. The cocaine inside of it does. Somebody is desperate to get it back and will do anything."

With a very Gallic shrug, she protested, "But I don't have it. How can I make that known?"

Linda interrupted smoothly. "At this point, we hope the criminals don't know you don't have it. We want them to show their hand."

Irene voiced my thought. "You're using me, endangering my life, as bait?"

"Not really. I doubt you would be safe even if they knew. And how would we let them know? We don't know who they are. And we don't know if they will blame you for the loss of the cocaine. They are probably not above revenge. Until we arrest the guilty, we have to keep you safe."

Linda's words and tone were so serious that she spooked me, although from the look on her face, Irene was unmoved. A cold chill crept up the back of my neck, and I was sure someone was watching us. The same feeling I'd had when I first spotted Janis Simmons or whoever she was. I looked around the vast lobby, craning my neck to look into far corners. It was almost empty, since we were the only guests who expected tea at an awkward hour. A couple sat on a loveseat, holding hands, their heads thrown back as they stared at the ceiling. A lone man in a wing chair was hidden by the newspaper he held in front of him. Like Simone/Janis hiding behind the menu. I decided Linda would think I was silly, so I said nothing.

Maybe it was divine intervention, but Ray Peterman showed up just as Irene was about to launch into another tirade, and she instantly became charming and pleasant. Apparently, he had met Linda at dinner the night before. Ray gave no hint how the dinner had gone as he asked Irene about the taping and then, before she could answer, greeted everyone individually, treating Linda as an old friend and introducing himself to Randy, who insisted on sitting slightly apart and not having tea and sandwiches.

I, on the other hand, ate so many tea sandwiches I was almost embarrassed, but I love smoked salmon almost as much as lobster. Murder and cocaine became the things that we talked around as we discussed the weather and Patrick's injured friend and our wedding. I desperately wished my family were here, but I assumed they were having a good time wherever they were. And Patrick! Maybe he'd know intuitively where I was and surprise me. Otherwise, I seemed stuck at tea as long as Irene wanted to stay.

Fortunately, she didn't want to spend the afternoon. About three thirty, she announced, "Raymond, I'd like to go to Neiman's. I need a new purse."

"Of course," he said, rising to his feet.

Linda rose too, but Irene waved a hand as though she would push her back into her seat. "You can stay here. Raymond will see that I am safe."

I watched this battle of the wills with little doubt about who would win. Irene could be forceful. But so, I suspected, could Linda, and I cheered silently when she said firmly "I am going with you" and rose from her seat.

"It's her job," Ray said placatingly, while offering Irene his arm. They departed, leaving Randy and me.

"I want to go home," I said.

On the way home, with Randy driving, I called Patrick, but he didn't answer, so I figured he was on his way back. Anyone who answers a cell phone while driving on the Outer Drive should have his or her head examined. We hadn't been in my apartment five minutes when Patrick walked in, with a cheerful, "Henny?"

His happiness toned down a bit when he glimpsed Randy lounging on the couch. Randy immediately jumped to his feet, and Patrick looked from him to me. Then he, who is usually the soul of hospitality, held out one hand and said, "You must be Randy." But he said it with no inflection, no warmth in his voice. It was the first time I'd ever seen my special Patrick unfriendly, even verging on anger.

"Patrick, as I told you last night, Randy is my protection for a few days until they find whoever killed Janis Simmons. He'll be with us all the time." I wrapped my arms around his neck, but he remained stiff.

"I can take care of Henny now. Thanks for keeping her safe, Randy." He reminded me of Irene dismissing Linda, and I almost laughed at the idea that Patrick could in any way act like Irene.

Randy cleared his throat. "Sorry, pal, but I can't leave until I get orders. I'll just wait outside. Give you all some privacy."

It wasn't as though I was going to rush Patrick into the bedroom, though that thought did occur to me. But there is a certain intimacy about being alone, even when recounting murderous events, that would disappear with the presence of a third party.

"You can wait in my apartment," Patrick said. "It's the one next door."

"Uh, no. The hall will be fine. I might miss someone coming up the stairs if I were in your apartment. It'll be okay."

But I knew it would be rude and ungrateful to send him out into the hall. "Nonsense," I said. "You can fill in any details if I miss them."

Patrick began to recover his normal, easygoing attitude. Maybe it was the mental vision of Randy sitting in the tiny hall, staring at the faded wallpaper. "Of course. You can't sit on the floor in the hall, and there's no room for a chair. We promise not to embarrass you." He ended with a fake leer at me, and then asked, "What's happened since we talked yesterday?"

I decided it would embarrass Patrick if I brought up his parents in front of Randy. The fewer people who knew about their attitude—ah, his mom's attitude—the less tension there might be when she was present. "Did I tell you that Janis Simmons apparently wasn't the woman killed at the Palmer House? The victim was a woman named Simone Guillaume. Schmidt thinks, though, that the real Janis Simmons is probably dead too. He says this means these people will not hesitate to kill again."

"But if they know the police are involved, they'll know the police have the cocaine and not you or Irene," Patrick protested.

"Not necessarily. They probably think the police are investigating the murder of Janis Simmons. And if that's true, they feel safe. My theory is that they killed the Simmons woman so this Simone whatever could take her place, and then Simone got scared, wanted out of being a—what do you call it?"

"Mule," Randy supplied.

"Right, mule. So she switched the purses."

"Or maybe they intended for her to make that switch all the time. Then they could steal the cocaine from Irene, and they would have safely gotten it into this country." Patrick loved making up theories like this.

Randy, I noticed, sat quietly and let us spin out our ideas. But when I brought up the identity question, he had a quick answer. I said I didn't understand how Simone Guillaume looked like the woman on Janis Simmons' driver's license, and Randy quickly interjected, "Driver's licenses are the easiest things in the world to doctor. I guess you never wanted a license saying you were twenty-one when you were only seventeen."

Patrick chuckled just a bit. "I never had a fake ID but I knew lots of kids who did."

I was not to be deterred from my theories as an armchair detective. "They may still plan to steal the cocaine from Irene, and that's why she is in more danger than I am. But why kill Simone?"

Randy spoke again. "Maybe they found her annoying or got tired of her."

"And they'd kill her for almost no reason?" I was incredulous.

Randy shrugged. "Some people don't need a reason or an excuse to kill."

Now that was another chilling thought.

My fear escalated when Irene called a bit later, her voice shaking with hysteria. "I don't know why you had to get married in this city," she exclaimed, and I thought, *Oh, swell. Whatever it is, it's my fault.*

"What are you talking about, Irene?"

"This man . . . right there in Neiman Marcus . . . he almost grabbed me. Linda said he was about to, but Raymond stopped him."

"Whoa! Start at the beginning." My heart was racing, and I tried calm myself with the thought that if she was calling me, she was okay. But every time I tried to ask something, she kept babbling. Finally, I said, "Put Linda on the phone, please."

In a minute, Linda came on. "We're safe, Henny. We're back in the hotel room. But it was scary for all of us. A man tried to kidnap Irene right there in the luggage department of Neiman's. But I had my eye on him all along. He was watching us while we were at tea."

"The man behind the newspaper," I breathed.

"Yep, that was him. I've talked to Detective Schmidt, and he's coming to the hotel, along with a stenographer, to take down detailed testimony. From me and Mrs. Foxglove." She hesitated a minute. "The versions may differ dramatically."

If there had been any laughter in me, I'd have giggled at the idea of Irene and a detailed statement. But I was too stunned for laughter.

# Chapter Nine

I should have known Irene would not be satisfied with a detailed statement to law enforcement. She needed to tell her story to someone who she felt would sympathize with the awful trauma she'd just been through. And, of course, guess who that someone was.

My family had gathered at my apartment after a long day at the Art Institute. There were raves ranging from "That place is amazing" to "Do you realize we just saw the real, the original of Monet's *Water Lilies?*" Janie was almost unable to stop talking about those lilies.

And then, of course, there was the food in the museum's upscale restaurant. Mom stuck to her lobster, this time in a salad, while Dad had a pasta with wild boar in a red sauce, and Janie had a sauce with shrimp, mussels, and calamari. I was proud of those Texans for branching out beyond what they usually ate. Ellie couldn't get beyond a hamburger, but I attributed her lack of culinary adventure to age. Mom splurged in the gift shop and got Dad some Edward Hopper socks—and T-shirts, with the iconic lion, for herself, the girls, and me. Then she was embarrassed she had not brought Patrick anything, but he hugged her and said, "You are giving me Henny. What more could I ask for?"

*Be still my heart.*

We were all talking at once—they were, and I was listening. I wasn't quite ready to share my day—when there was a demanding knock on the door, and Irene burst into my kitchen. Note to self: learn to lock the door. I still would have answered but at least I'd have had a nanosecond to prepare. She was followed by a sheepish Linda Rutledge, who looked at me and sort of shrugged. I got the message: she had tried to stop Irene but couldn't. Somewhere along the way they had dropped Ray Peterman.

Randy, who as usual was sitting somewhat apart in a corner, sat up and took interest.

Irene had never been to my apartment before, and she stopped, stunned apparently, at the small size. "This is where you cook?" she asked incredulously.

As I nodded, she waved a hand in the air, dismissing that topic with, "No matter, I must tell you what happened today. You are lucky I lived to tell the tale." She wiped a dramatic hand across her forehead.

An awkward silence had come over my family, who knew nothing about tea at the Palmer House or the aborted shopping trip to Neiman's. They stared at Irene, barely managing to avoid the open mouths of disbelief. She never noticed. "A murderer—*muertier*—nearly grabbed me right there in Neiman Marcus. I was looking at purses, minding my own business, and this hand strong as iron attached itself to my arm. I have the bruises from it, like a handprint on my upper arm." She was talking rapidly, as though high herself on something, and she started to roll back her sleeve, which was too tight for that. She'd have had to undress to show us, something I wanted to forestall.

"Amazing, Irene!" I almost shouted to distract her.

"I turned quickly, of course, and found myself staring into the face of evil." A dramatic pause, during which she clasped her hand to her chest as though quieting her racing heart. "His face was hidden behind all kinds of growth that he should have shaved off, but his eyes…. I will never forget them. They will haunt me the rest of my days. Evil and cold and dark. He never said anything, just held my arm in this iron grip."

"And then what?" Ellie asked, breathless. I think she thought she was at a crime movie.

"Raymond saved the day. He stuck out a foot and tripped that beastly man. Were it not for him, who knows where I'd be this minute? Probably at the bottom of the Chicago River."

Ellie gasped, and I tried to silence her with a long look. It didn't work. "Did he get away?" she asked.

Irene sat down suddenly in a kitchen chair, apparently overwhelmed by her own emotions. Mom, Dad, and Janie were too overcome by the dramatic performance to say anything, and Linda still stood awkwardly by the door. She probably felt like an intruder. I also thought she probably had more of a hand in saving Irene than Ray Peterman did, but I kept quiet.

Patrick was the one who went to Irene, put a caring hand on her shoulder, and said softly, "We're so grateful you're here with us, safe."

I flinched at that, wondering if she really was safe. Irene, meanwhile, reached a hand up to pat his on her shoulder and said, "Thank you, dear boy." Then, to the room at large, "Raymond has gone home to recover. The excitement exhausted him."

I wanted to sidle over to Linda and get her version of the story, but there was no tactful way to do that. Slowly, everyone began to talk at once. Irene moved to the couch, and the others clustered around her. It was my chance.

Linda simply whispered, "I couldn't use my gun in that crowded store, and I had to choose between chasing the guy and staying with Mrs. Foxglove. I thought that was my responsibility. And no, Mr. Peterman did not trip him. He stumbled over his own feet, far as I can tell. They're not smart. If they'd have had two men, she'd be gone."

Randy had come to stand by us and hear Linda's story. I thought he looked a bit jealous that she got the action he'd been longing for.

That straightforward explanation had much more impact on me than all Irene's dramatics. To put it simply, I was terrified to realize what kind of people were threatening us, and I was even more grateful for Randy and that gun tucked in the back of his waistband. I wanted to offer everyone coffee or tea, but for a bit my hands were too shaky for that. So I had what my mother would later call one of my "harebrained ideas."

Clapping my hands together, which kept them from shaking, I commanded attention. "Everyone has had a long, difficult day, and we were just talking about getting Chinese takeout. I'm sure Patrick will go pick it up for us."

Patrick looked surprised for a minute but then had the grace to smile. "Of course." Belatedly, I remembered the spaghetti sauce in Patrick's refrigerator. Well, we'd just freeze it—or use it tomorrow, if the world hadn't fallen apart by then.

"Rather than take everyone's orders, which will confuse me and the restaurant, I'm going to get large orders of three or four things, like beef and broccoli. We have plenty of drinks." Turning to the diva, I asked, "You will stay, Irene?"

She looked blank. "Chinese? I couldn't. No, I must get back to Raymond. Linda, you must drive me."

Poor Linda. I bet she would have liked some takeout. As it was, she dutifully followed Irene, with an apologetic glance over her shoulder.

I ordered beef with broccoli, Kung Pao tofu, figuring my family had never eaten tofu, orange chicken, shrimp fried rice, and egg rolls. Mom had probably had enough lobster, although I didn't ask her. We got enough food to feed an army, which is what I was beginning to feel we were. Everybody ate heartily, and as I expected, my family was underwhelmed by tofu. While Ellie thought it was too spicy, the rest balked at the consistency. We ate silently, and talk dwindled after that. Everyone was tired—if not before, now worn out by Irene's drama. By eight, Patrick and I were shepherding them out the door.

Randy had authoritatively said the girls should spend the night again at Best Western, where Schmidt would station someone to watch over them, and my folks, shocked by the bare truth behind Irene's story, agreed. Randy clinched it by adding, "Besides, Patrick is back now, and needs his apartment."

After they left, Randy said apologetically, "I'm going to have to spend the night, but right now I'm going to go sit on the steps outside your door. I want to talk to my girlfriend privately." With a grin, he went out the door.

Patrick and I fell into each other's arms, and I got the first good kiss I'd gotten since he came home. Almost as if on cue, the phone rang. Caller ID said Detective Schmidt, so of course I answered. Patrick just shrugged and plopped himself on my couch.

"Got a report from Aix-en-Provence. Janis Simmons is, er was, a Brit working there. Her family has been unable to contact her for about two weeks now. They sent a photo, but it doesn't look anything like the woman who was killed. Or the woman on that driver's license, who is clearly Simone Guillaume. Just to be sure, I've asked for a DNA samples for both women. But I suspect we'll never find poor Janis."

From the sound over the phone, he paused to take a long drag on his cigarette, and I pictured Schmidt in his tiny office with its dirt-streaked windows. Before I could comment on the probable murder of Janis Simmons, he went on. "Simone Guillaume, on the other hand, called Aix-en-Provence home but had been living in a small town. What's the town Mrs. Foxglove said she was from?"

"Peyrolles-en-Provence," I supplied.

"That's it!" This time he sounded triumphant. "It's a really small town, isn't it?" When I said yes, he came to the logical conclusion. "So they almost definitely knew each other. Here's what I think. Simone hung out some at that café, and she and Mrs. Foxglove were friends, if not chummy. Mrs. F. probably mentioned that she was coming to Chicago. And, yes, Simone was on the same flight—but she booked as Janis Simmons, flew coach, and did something—who knows what?—so Mrs. F. didn't see her. A disguise of some sort."

I took a deep breath. "But does that put us any closer to knowing who killed her and who might be after Irene?" In my mind I added, or *me*.

Patrick looked a question at me, raising his eyebrows and holding out his hands, palms up, in the classic "I don't know" gesture. A one-sided conversation must have been terribly frustrating for him.

Schmidt was quiet for a long minute, and I was just about to mouth something to Patrick, when the detective finally said, "No, it doesn't. But I've got a couple of theories. This Simone woman was hired as a mule to transport the cocaine, whether specifically to Chicago or not, we can't be sure. But she either thought the people who hired her might kill her rather than pay up, or that some rival dealers would kill her before she could deliver. Either way, I'm going to have to work with law enforcement in Provence."

"So why Irene?"

"If she knew her at the café, as I suspect, she'd have seen that Mrs. F. is a perfect target—easily flattered, unsophisticated about some things, not likely to be suspicious. I couldn't have picked a better decoy myself. I suspect Simone thought the transfer would be temporary, and she could use her friendship with Mrs. F. to get the drug purse back when it was safe."

"There is someone who would know if they were friends," I said hesitantly. I knew what would happen when I said the name. "Gabrielle."

At that name, Patrick got up and began to pace impatiently. So unlike my nice, calm Patrick.

I heard hands being clapped together. "Of course, the daughter! You must call her immediately—well, wait until it's a decent hour over there. I always get confused by the time differences."

Sigh. Gabrielle was the last person I wanted to talk to. She'd probably decide she must come to Chicago right away to save her mother. That would be the woman she spent the first twenty years of her life rebelling against.

Patrick, meanwhile, was making frantic gestures. Much as I would have liked to believe he wanted to resume the kissing part of our reunion, after a brief two days apart, I knew what he wanted was to hear what Schmidt had been saying.

"I'll let you know what she says" was all I could muster for Al Schmidt.

Before he hung up, he said, "You know, I still might have to hire you. 'Course you'd need some training. And you'd have to give up this cooking business."

"Thanks," I said, "but I'm happiest in the kitchen." Just then I fervently wished that cooking was all that I had on my mind. And Patrick and a wedding, of course.

I turned to Patrick after ending the call and said decisively, "It all traces back to Provence, and I am one hundred percent sure that Chance Charpentier is behind this. He's been masquerading as a good guy for Irene and Gabrielle, but all the while he's running a drug smuggling operation and planning to use mother and daughter who knows how else. After all, we know he was the one behind Gabrielle's kidnapping last year. He just never was caught, and his"—I searched for the words—"henchman took the fall for him."

Patrick at first was amused. "You're really learning the lingo, aren't you, Henny. First mule, now henchman and take the fall." But he turned serious. "This is not a romance novel with a murder. You don't really know that Chance was behind Gabrielle's kidnapping. He's in France, and we're in Chicago, where the point is to keep Irene safe, not determine whether or not Chance Charpentier is guilty of anything from kidnapping to smuggling."

I stared at him. He was so wrong.

# Chapter Ten

My family wanted Chicago dogs for lunch, but it took them a long time to get dressed and organized. On the other hand, Patrick and I had been up half the night, hashing over what had happened since he left, what Schmidt had said on the phone about the late Simone Guillaume, and my absolute certainty that Chance Charpentier was behind the whole thing. I could picture him, no longer the suave, young, slim, and attractive heir but now the aging patron behind an organized criminal network. He would now have a paunch, walk with a slight limp (gout from overindulgence, maybe), and have a comb-over in a vain attempt to hide his increasing baldness. My imagination ran away with me, though I didn't share that description with Patrick.

We were both too wired to sleep in, and by eight o'clock we were sitting at my kitchen table with cups of coffee. Randy sat on the couch cradling his cup of coffee and did his best to ignore us.

"Breakfast?" I asked. "There's leftover Chinese."

Patrick shuddered. "Toast. Nothing else."

So, I toasted some good rye bread and moved the butter keeper, with soft butter for spreading, from the counter to the table. And we sat there staring at each other, dumbfounded by the situation we found ourselves in. The wedding we'd so carefully planned had turned into a remote dream, and instead murder was an up-close mess. And cocaine. How could I forget that?

"Should I tell the hotel we may have to cancel?" I stirred my coffee.

Patrick looked aghast. "We made a huge down payment. We'll lose it if we cancel."

I just shrugged. It was, I thought, what it was. We were caught in something beyond our control, something much bigger than us.

He switched topics. "How much did Schmidt say that cocaine was worth?"

Shaking my head, I said, "He didn't say. I didn't ask. Why? You thinking we could use it to pay for the wedding?" I was kidding, at least I thought I was.

Patrick was now indignant. "Henny!"

I got up and went to wrap my arms around his shoulders. "I'm sorry. I didn't mean that the way it came out. Of course, I know we can't do that. I just want things to work out."

"This is Thursday morning," he reminded me. "The wedding is three days away."

"Four, depending on how you count. We've got all day today."

And that's when Dad called to say they all wanted Chicago dogs and where should they go. A Chicago dog is not just any old hot dog like you'd get at a baseball park. It's very specific: an all-beef frankfurter on a poppy-seed bun, topped with yellow mustard, chopped white onions, sweet pickle relish, a dill pickle spear, tomato slices or wedges, and pickled sport peppers, which are too hot for me and would kill Ellie. Add a dash of celery salt and see if you can fit it all in your mouth. It has so many toppings that cooks talk about it being "dragged through the garden." Personally, I'm not fond of them—too many pickles and peppers. I like sauerkraut on my hot dogs, but I didn't think I could talk them into Berghoff's.

"I guess Nathan's," I said. "It's between where you are and where we are, so we could meet there. Between Dorchester and Kenwood on Fifty-Third. You're on your own about parking."

We agreed to meet at eleven thirty, after which they wanted to go to the Museum of Science and Industry. Ellie had heard about Colleen Moore's Fairy Castle and wanted to see it. Dad wanted to go down in the coal mine, which I had always thought would make me claustrophobic.

No one mentioned Irene—not Patrick, not Dad, not Randy. But there was no way I could avoid thinking about her. Getting up to rinse coffee cups, I said, "I suppose I should call Irene."

Patrick stretched and yawned. "I don't know. You know what they say about no news, and it sure is more peaceful without her. But you really should call Gabrielle." He looked at his watch. "Should be midafternoon over there."

"Yeah," I persisted, "but Irene was so worried about Ray Peterman last night, I wonder . . ."

He interrupted me. "Have you thought about that guy? I mean I only met him that once and he seemed nice enough, sort of old-fashioned or maybe I mean European. But the way he latched on to Irene right away. I can't help but wonder if the whole thing was some scheme and he knew about it . . ."

"I believe they had an old friend in common. Gabrielle's grandfather. And they were corresponding. He knew she was coming."

"Chance's father?"

I nodded. "Guess I better get it over with and call Irene."

Irene was not exactly distraught, but she was having a pity party all by herself, though I assumed Linda Rutledge was still with her. "Raymond has what he calls an obligation, so I have nothing to do all day."

When I told her we were going to eat hot dogs and then go to the museum and she was welcome to join us, I could practically hear her shudder over the phone. "No, absolutely not. I do not eat hot dogs."

I was not going to suggest that Nathan's offered other things.

Irene was silent for a moment and then said, "I might go to the museum. That might be amusing."

In the background, Linda said something, and Irene apparently turned to her and said, loudly enough that I could hear it, "I will not be held prisoner. I will go where I want."

"You talk to Linda," I said. "I'll check with you after lunch." I hung up before she could say anything else. Part of me wanted to tell Linda I was sorry she was missing the hot dog outing.

I was about to call Gabrielle when I realized not only was I dumb about international calls, I didn't have Gabrielle's number. If there was an information number in France, no matter how difficult, it would still be easier than calling Irene back and asking. So I called up an operator in the States, not easy to do with automated systems. In fact, I suspected the man I got was in India or the Philippines but not the States. After I plowed through his accent, he was helpful. I said I wanted the number for Café Gabrielle in Peyrolles-en-Provence, and after a bit he explained about the code for international calls and the number for France. I dutifully wrote down 011 followed by 33. And then he reeled off a string of nine numbers that left me scrambling to keep up. I read them back to him, and by some miracle I had gotten them all in the right order.

I took a deep breath, looked at Patrick for encouragement, and dialed. The phone only rang once before a bright and very young-sounding voice said, "Bonjour. Ici Bernadette."

I waffled. My French was nonexistent, so I tried, "Hi, Bernadette. Is Gabrielle there?"

"Pardonnez moi?"

Clearly, I hadn't hit on the right way to do this. Patrick literally grabbed the phone from me. "Je m'appelle Patrick," he said fluently. "Je voudrais parler Gabrielle."

I was awestruck. I heard some words on the other end, only because my ear was practically in Patrick's face. He gently pushed me away and said, "Oui. Je rappellerai. Merci." And he clicked to end the call.

"She's not in."

"I didn't know you speak French. Why didn't you tell me?"

He grinned, his eyes twinkling with amusement. "Because you and I had no need to speak French. English did very well for us." Then he sobered. "She wasn't in, and my French isn't good enough to explore where she went and when she'll be back."

My devious mind had a plan. "Perfect. I'll give Schmidt the number, and he can call later. I'll just explain we have a full day planned. Besides, he'll probably do better with her than I would."

And that's just what I did. Left Detective Schmidt a message with the number and said I'd check with him when we got back to the apartment.

Nathan's was in an older building, tucked in between other stores, with apartments above. Inside it had the counter where you ordered with offerings displayed on overhead boards, like a McDonald's or something. But the difference ended there—the food was either Jamaican or American, a strangely split offering to me, and I never paid attention to the Jamaican menu. But on the American menu you could order several toppings on your hot dog, or a burger, salad, pasta, seafood—so much that I sometimes wished they had focused on the hot dogs and the "Chicago style" items which were heavy on sausage but also included a Reuben.

All six of us slid into one of the larger, circular booths, left over, I suspected, from when the space was a beloved neighborhood coffee shop. Everybody studied the menu and most, including Patrick and Randy, opted for the Chicago dog. I chose the Polish dog because it had sauerkraut, and Dad stubbornly insisted on a Reuben.

"I've eaten enough hot dogs watching the Texas Rangers," he said.

Ellie, with her crush on Randy, turned to him and asked, "You will go to the museum, won't you?"

He shook his head. "No, ma'am. I'm going to ask Henny not to go either. I don't think it would be easy to protect her there, with the crowds. If somebody grabbed Mrs. Foxglove in Neiman's, they could snatch Henny at the museum."

Ellie pouted, but I tried to be practical. "They could snatch me here." I pointed out that I was sitting on the open end of the booth and would soon go to the restroom.

"No, ma'am. Won't happen. I've checked the place."

I did notice him lingering at the counter and taking in the entire restaurant, which wasn't that big.

My family had apparently gotten their second wind after their exhaustion of the previous night. They ate their hot dogs and whatever in record time and were impatient to head to the museum. My feelings were just a bit hurt that they said nothing more than a casual "sorry you can't go with us" to Patrick and me. They did agree to meet us at the apartment at five thirty to plan our evening.

Patrick was deep in conversation with Randy and barely waved at my family as they trooped out the door. Finally, the two of them came back to the booth where I sat, and Patrick said cheerfully, "Let's go back to the apartment."

"What are we going to do all afternoon?" I asked in a fit of self-pity. A part of me said there surely must be a thousand and one things I needed to do to prepare for the wedding, but nothing seemed urgent. Until Irene was safe, we were in a holding pattern.

"I have an idea," Patrick said, "but we have to go back to the apartment."

Randy just smiled at him and climbed behind the wheel of the car.

Once we were there, Randy said, "Listen, you two, I'm just gonna sit here and watch television. I don't think any drug dealers will come busting through the door, but if they do, I'm ready. And I need to check in with Lieutenant Schmidt, and my girlfriend will wonder if I've fallen off the face of the earth."

I looked at Patrick. "Want to ride bikes to Promontory Point and check out the shelter, make sure it's clean?"

He looked horrified. "Without Randy? Of course, we can't do that. You're just crotchety and tired because neither of us slept well last night. Come on, you need a nap." He took me by the hand, led me to the bedroom, and closed the door firmly.

We had a lovely afternoon. Both our phones were unplugged, and I never gave another thought to what Irene was doing or my family exploring the museum without me. After all, I'd already been there.

When my family arrived at five thirty, Patrick and I were both refreshed, showered, and dressed in clean clothes. While we poured wine and soft drinks, poor Randy snuck into the shower. I thought he must be awfully tired, since he didn't get a nap.

The family, particularly my sisters, were full of all they'd seen and done. "The Colleen Moore dollhouse is unbelievable, Henny! You've got to see it. All that detail in miniature. I want Dad to build me a dollhouse." Ellie clapped her hands in excitement.

Mom quirked an eyebrow. "Aren't you a little old?"

Not to be outdone, Janie chimed in with praise for the re-creation of a downtown Chicago street at the turn of the century, complete with Marshall Field & Co., a dentist's office, a corset shop, and even an early automobile in which Janie and Ellie posed for a picture that was printed in sepia tones.

To Dad's dismay, the coal mine was closed, but he found some of the space exhibits fascinating, and they all said they wanted a second visit.

"Except tomorrow, we're going on the architectural river tour." Mom seemed more interested in that than she had the museum itself. I'd taken that tour when I first came to Chicago and it was pretty impressive, with a knowledgeable guide explaining what you were seeing.

"And Adele and her parents are coming with us," Ellie added.

Of course, I bit. "Who's Adele?"

"This really cute girl. I think she's about eight. She and her parents are staying at our motel, and we ran into them at the museum and struck up a conversation. She's really impressed that you're on television, says she wants to be a chef when she grows up. You'll meet her. And her parents wanted to know all about Irene and how you came to be on TV. They're really nice people."

Mom chimed in. "After raising you three, I really am a sucker for little girls. This one is extra cute and smart, and I liked her parents too. They think you're a celebrity, Henny, but the one they really want to meet is Irene. In fact, Emily Parker was pretty insistent about meeting Irene, so I told her about the signing tomorrow night."

I laughed nervously. Anybody who thought I was a celebrity, or even that Irene was, must be pretty naïve. But I also had a practical concern. "I'm sure I'll like them, but you didn't invite them to the wedding, did you?"

Ellie looked away. "No, really no. I just told them when it would be in the lobby. They might come watch, like spectators. They were so intrigued by the wedding, they wanted to know all about the plans."

All I needed was to have a crowd gather when I'd assured Jim Holcomb, the general manager of the Palmer House, that we'd be unobtrusive and discreet. Briefly it occurred to me that the Parkers now knew our entire itinerary, but then I was distracted by Patrick, who reached over and took my hand in his. Maybe he wanted me to stop wringing my hands. Trust Patrick. What did he say? "I'm sure Adele is an interesting kid. We'll enjoy meeting her."

I hadn't checked missed calls for when we had our phones turned off, but I should have known better. The minute I sat down with a glass of wine and began to ask dinner preferences, Irene called. She was obviously riding her high horse.

"Where have you been? I've called you all afternoon?" she shrilled.

I didn't confess that I hadn't check missed calls, hadn't even given it a thought. "Irene! What can I do for you?" That was Henny the helpful.

"Find Raymond," she shouted. "He's disappeared."

"Ray Peterman has disappeared?" I echoed. "Surely he's just busy."

"Surely not," she snapped. "He's not at home, not at the hotel, and he doesn't answer his cell phone. I'm afraid he's in trouble."

That tiny blip in your brain that precedes real dread hit me softly. "When did you last hear from him?" I asked.

"This morning, when he told me he'd be busy in the morning. He did not say all day." She had gone from shrill to crisp and businesslike, and I could imagine her drumming that left hand, tremor and all, on the table.

"What does Linda say?"

She made a sound like "Pfft," and her voice rose a bit, now in anger. "All Linda says is I can't do this, and I can't do that, and I am tired of her."

Linda, I knew, was sitting right there hearing every word. Fortunately, she had caught on to Irene pretty quickly and was not swayed by her insults.

"May I talk to her?" I asked as politely as I could.

"I don't know what good that will do, but here . . ." I could hear her say dismissively, "She wants to talk to you," and in a moment, Linda was on the phone.

"I've told Mrs. Foxglove that it's too early to be alarmed. She wanted to call the hospitals, even file a missing person's report. But I told her people generally are missing twenty-four hours before we do that." She spoke in a calm, controlled voice, and I wished fervently that some of that calm would rub off on Irene.

"Should you call Lieutenant Schmidt?"

"I already did," she said, "at Mrs. Foxglove's urging."

I could imagine the tone of the urging.

"He supported what I told her."

Changing the scene seemed to be the only solution right now, so I said, "My family is just beginning to talk about supper. Would you like to meet us?"

"Thank you, but I'm sure we'll stay here and wait to hear. Mrs. Foxglove may not even be hungry. Oh, and one other thing. The lieutenant is giving Randy and me tomorrow off. There will be substitutes."

"Now? When everything's so unsettled? I mean, we've got a wedding in three days."

"That's why we're getting twenty-four hours off now," she said evenly.

Linda Rutledge was nobody's fool. And her warning had come just in time. Not ten minutes later Randy answered a knock on the door and ushered in a uniformed woman.

"Skylar Calhoun," he announced. "She'll be your new protection until this time tomorrow night."

Without another word, Randy slipped out the door. It dawned on me I wasn't sure about his last name—Collins?—and I had no idea how to reach him except through Schmidt's office. I felt somehow abandoned.

# Chapter Eleven

Skylar Calhoun had one of the shortest haircuts I've ever seen on a woman. She was barely as tall as I am and much stockier. She also looked like she worked out every day. Truth was she looked more like a guy than a girl.

Patrick's mouth fell open, and I could tell he barely stopped himself in time from saying, "A woman?" I kicked him under the kitchen table, and he turned his expression into a smile. "Glad to have you with us, Skylar. What an unusual name."

"It's a nonbinary name," she said in a matter-of-fact way.

"Let me introduce everyone," I said, picking up my role as Little Miss Cheerful. I went around the room, and they all nodded or smiled or gave silly little half waves.

"How many are staying here tonight?" she asked, taking out a small notebook.

"Just Patrick and me," I said, and my mom jumped in with "Patrick has his own apartment next door." Thanks, Mom.

Skylar nodded, said "Good," and made a note in her book.

I looked at Patrick, but he just shook his head ever so slightly.

Dad, bless him, sensed the tension and said, "I'm hungry. What are we going to do about dinner?"

"How about Valois?" I asked. "It's a pretty famous cafeteria on Fifty-Third Street. The Obama family is said to eat there when they're in town. It's a cafeteria with sandwiches and salads, but they have daily specials like baked chicken and roast beef."

"Down-home food," my dad pronounced.

"Yep, American cooking," I said. Every time I went to Valois, I picked up a new idea for my TV show, usually something basic like baked pork chops that were moist and tender instead of the too-often dry and tough. I was still wondering if I could approximate their liver and onions and then get away with a show about liver. I could only imagine Bob's reaction.

"Let's go," Dad said heartily, and there was a flurry of women combing their hair and putting on lipstick.

Skylar had dragged a kitchen chair to the edge of the living room, ostentatiously out of the conversation circle. Now she announced, "Ms. James, you will stay here, of course."

"Of course not," I flared. "This is my family, and we're going to dinner. You will go with us." That was an ultimatum, but I knew then it was going to be a long twenty-four hours.

Without an ounce of grace, she agreed if I would ride in her car. Everyone else, even Patrick, was on their own, and she made that clear. Patrick nodded his head at me, so I agreed. Skylar's car turned out to be a Jeep—I could have predicted that. She drove in a certain precise manner that I decided characterized everything she did. But she wasn't slow, and we arrived at Valois before the others.

Valois is an unpretentious restaurant, its walls adorned with framed newspaper write-ups and signed photographs of such famous diners as Barack Obama and former Chicago Mayor Harold Washington. We waited so everyone could go through the line together, and Dad graciously picked up the check. I said a silent prayer of gratitude that prices at Valois are so reasonable and the food so good.

Skylar declined an invitation to eat with us, but she surely arranged the seating. There were so many of us, we sat in a circular booth, and I was right in the middle with no possibility of getting out if I wanted to. I was also not next to Patrick, which frustrated me a bit. I supposed she thought that middle position would make it harder for someone to snatch me. She, of course, planted herself in a chair at the edge of the table, facing away from us as she continually scanned the restaurant. All we saw was her back, but that had its benefits.

To my surprise, Mom, Janie, and Ellie had chicken fajitas. I wanted to tell them they could eat fajitas, probably better ones, any time in Texas, and they should order some Midwestern food. I frowned at the Florida grouper because we were a really long distance from Florida, and I decided not to try liver and onions—I couldn't devote my attention to it. Talk about unimaginative—I had a cheeseburger. Dad and Patrick ate like hearty men—the roast beef plate dinner.

Before I even got a bite of my cheeseburger, my phone rang. Ordinarily, I would have either excused myself from the table or punched the "Can't talk right now" button, but there was no way I could get out except by disrupting everyone, and the caller was John Wilson, Irene's lawyer.

"Irene has called and told me to deliver an ultimatum to Lieutenant Schmidt," he said without preamble.

"What kind of ultimatum?"

"Find Raymond Peterman now or else." He sounded weary. One of John Wilson's talents was apparently mimicry, because I could hear Irene's tone in his voice.

"I won't even ask what the else is about," I said.

"Don't. I'm on my way now to have dinner with her and the policewoman. I understand we'll be dining in her room. Just how I wanted to spend my evening." He paused a minute. "I just thought you should know. I'll do my best to calm her, but I thought I'd warn you. It may be a long evening."

"It already is," I said, knowing he wouldn't understand. I thanked him and went back to my cheeseburger, which now tasted like straw.

As we broke up after supper, my family headed to the motel, and Skylar and I to the apartment. I realized Patrick was stranded. The only way to deal with Skylar was to issue an order: Patrick would ride with us. Skylar gave in, but I could tell she thought I was usurping her authority. We rode in an uncomfortable silence.

Once at the apartment, I made it clear one more time that this was my home, and I was in charge. Bustling around for clean sheets,

I made up a bed on the couch, while Skylar sat in the chair she'd commandeered for her own and Patrick stood watching me with a bemused expression on his face. Then I poured two glasses of wine, handed one to Patrick, and said to Skylar, "We're going to bed now. You can brush your teeth in the bathroom in Patrick's apartment. Be sure to lock up."

She opened her mouth, but no sound came out as she watched Patrick follow me into the bedroom. He gave a kind of half wave over his shoulder, murmured, "'Night," and I managed not to slam the door. Of course, my clever scheme meant that instead of sitting comfortably in the living room, we sat Indian style on the bed as we hashed over the evening.

Normally, I would have exploded, but I was acutely aware that Skylar was probably listening at the door. "She is really unsufferable," I whispered.

Patrick looked away. "What's that old saying? Never judge a man until you've walked a mile in his moccasins."

"Moccasins?" I giggled. "My mom always said shoes."

Ruefully, he said, "My mom never taught me any old sayings like that. I had to learn them when I was grown." As if reminded, he said, "My parents will be here tomorrow night." He didn't need to tell me. Joanna O'Malley had lurked in the back of my mind ever since Patrick came home from Winnetka, but she was a problem I'd temporarily put behind me. How would she act? How would I act? Nervous does not begin to describe my feelings. After all, I was going to be related to these people the rest of my life. That she didn't like me was bad enough, but what about once she found out about Simone Guillaume and the cocaine? And how would she take Irene?

Patrick sensed my thoughts. "It will be fine," he said, giving me a gentle kiss. "When I was up there, I sort of told them what's going on."

"How did you 'sort of' tell them?"

He laughed. "Okay. I told them. Everything I knew at the time, which I think is most of it except Mr. Peterman hadn't disappeared." Turning thoughtful, he asked, "What do you think happened to him?"

"Don't change the subject!" I almost snapped at poor, dear Patrick. "Your mom doesn't think I'm good enough for you—or at least she prefers your cousin, which is kinky. How am I going to tell my family that?"

"Don't tell them," he said softly. "It will never come up. Joanna O'Malley always, always behaves perfectly in public." He gave me another, longer kiss, but didn't let go of the topic. "What do you think happened to Ray Peterman?"

I wished I had an answer, but I didn't. The easy answers—kidnapped to ransom the drugs, killed in revenge—were things I didn't want to think about, something I can be skilled at. If I don't want to think about it, it goes to the back of my mind, just as Joanna had. Unfortunately, sometimes it percolates back there and comes forward to confront me. That's what happened when Patrick asked.

"I don't want to talk about it," I said.

"Henny, we may have to face some pretty tough stuff in the next couple of days. I want you to be prepared, not surprised." He rubbed my back gently, and I wanted to throw myself at him.

Instead, I managed to say, "I know we're dealing with bad people—they've apparently killed two women and tried to kidnap a third. But we don't seem any closer to finding them than we did four days ago when Irene discovered the cocaine in her purse. Sometimes those bad people seem sort of unreal to me."

"Don't ever let them seem so unreal you let your guard down, because, Henny, they are very real."

"I need to go to sleep," I said. "I've been cranky all day. I'm tired."

Far be it from Patrick to disagree with me. "So you have. Hope you feel better tomorrow."

I went to sleep cranky but with a vow to wake up happy. Still in the night, as I curled up against Patrick's comforting back, a thought kept niggling at me: if the bad guys, whoever they were, knew that police were protecting us, then they surely figured out that the police had the drugs. So what did they want?

And how much protection was Skylar Calhoun?

# Chapter Twelve

I did not wake up happy. I woke up tired, and it took me a minute to remember what was going on in my life, what I was to do today. It was Friday, and Mom and I planned to spend the morning making potato salad, a pot of pinto beans, and barbecue sauce for the rehearsal dinner. This evening was Irene's book signing. I'd have to call this morning and remind her, a chore I dreaded.

Only when my phone rang, did I realize that Irene had not called me all night. Did that mean Ray had reappeared? And Al Schmidt never called to report on his call to Gabrielle. I grabbed the phone quickly, hoping it wouldn't wake Patrick, who snored gently beside me.

It was Lieutenant Schmidt, which was sort of a relief. I had nothing to say to Irene that would be helpful.

"You awake?"

"Yes," I replied. "What's going on? Did you find Mr. Peterman?"

"Negative. I got nothing. No person, no body, but I got a note."

I couldn't tell if this made him angry, sad, or hopeful. To me, it meant we were moving off dead center. "What did it say?"

He took a deep breath. "Actually, Mrs. Foxglove got a note. It said, 'You're next.'"

Envisioning a note of pasted letters, I said, "I suppose you can't trace it."

"There are fingerprints, but no match in the databases so far. I suspect if there's a match anywhere, it's in France. Note was typed—but on an old manual typewriter. We'd have to run down every old typewriter in the city for a match."

"What does 'you're next' mean? Does that mean they've killed Ray Peterman and she's next?"

"Not necessarily. Could mean next after Simone Guillaume. But now it's twenty-four hours that Peterman has been missing, so I can officially declare him missing. I got no body, no note specifically about him, nothing really."

"And you have a frantic Irene Foxglove."

"She's gone from frantic to grief, convinced he's dead."

My phone jingled, signaling another incoming call. It was Irene. I ignored it, thinking I'd call back. "Irene's calling," I told Schmidt. "I'll call her back after we talk."

"I only got one other thing," he said. "Gabrielle called late last night, which would have been middle of the night or early morning in France. Confirmed that Simone was in the café a lot but said she didn't anything more about her. Simone and Mrs. F. were pals, sat and talked for hours."

"And yet Irene denies ever knowing her. Why? This is all too tangled."

"You're telling me."

My phone jingled again, and by this time Patrick was sitting up in bed, favoring me with unhappy looks. "I better take her call," I told Schmidt. "I'll call you later."

I punched the button and started to say good morning to Irene, but she interrupted me loudly. "He's home!" she shouted. "Raymond is all right. It was a false alarm."

My first instinct was to say that my nerves couldn't take many more false alarms. I did manage to say, "Thank heaven. I'm so relieved. What happened to him?"

Irene sighed. "He has a sister in Peoria—where is that place? *Peu importe.* This sister, she was sick, thought she was dying, so Raymond rushed to her bedside. Called her doctor, who convinced her she is not dying. She is, how you say it? *Nérveux!* But she has no other family. Raymond is it. He is *très apologétique* for worrying everyone."

Called to a sick sister! My head was spinning, but I managed to turn to Patrick and whisper, "Ray is okay." He flopped back down on the pillows. "Irene," I said sternly, "you must call Lieutenant Schmidt immediately, so he can call off the search."

"*Mais oui.* And I suppose he told you about the silly note I got."

"It's not silly," I muttered, but she had hung up.

Patrick and I wandered out of the bedroom in our pajamas and robes. Skylar was back in "her" chair, occupied with studying her cell phone. A glance in the kitchen sink told me she had fixed something to eat during the night. But why were there two cups and plates? Two snacks? Did she eat throughout the night? She looked up briefly in response to our cheerful greetings, and I thought she looked different. Maybe less detached, less remote. Surely that wasn't the beginning of a slight curve of the mouth—not a smile, mind you, just a curve.

Over toast and good, homemade peach jam, Patrick said he thought he'd go on the river cruise with my family. He also said his family would like to host mine for dinner at that evening. "Nothing fancy. Maybe The Lockwood . . ."

I reminded him tonight was Irene's signing at 57th Street Books. "Why not something local?" I asked. "We'll all be in Hyde Park, either at a hotel or the bookstore, so why go all the way downtown again?" I thought for a minute. "We haven't had your spaghetti sauce—I froze it—so how about Italian at Piccolo Mondo? It's close to all of us except my family's motel. But maybe they'll be at the signing."

"Good idea! I'll make reservations. Let's see . . ." He began to count on his fingers. "Nine, with Randy, who will be back with us by then, I presume. Should we include Irene and Ray? I think my folks want to meet her."

"That means Linda Rutledge too. Twelve people. That's asking a lot of your folks," I said.

"They can handle it," he said. "But I bet they skip the book signing. That's just how they are. Mom doesn't like to cook." He gave me a quick kiss and headed for his own apartment. In the doorway, he stopped and looked at Skylar.

"Okay if Henny comes to my apartment for a minute? We can leave both doors open."

She sighed, as if terribly imposed upon, but nodded. I didn't think she would have done that last night.

Once in his apartment, Patrick quietly confessed to what I'd begun to suspect.

"Skylar and I visited about three o'clock this morning. I made us each a PBJ sandwich." Pause. Deep breath. "She's pregnant, and she's scared."

Was he trying to fool me? "That's impossible!" I said it too loudly.

He put a finger to his lips, signaling me to lower my always-too-loud voice. "She was raped—some macho guy teaching her a lesson."

"That's awful. Did she report it?"

"Of course not," he almost snapped. "She just found out last week she's pregnant. She has no one to tell, no one to help her. She isn't exactly close to her family. In fact, they pretty much don't speak."

Not speaking to your family was one of the saddest things I could imagine, and I knew what Patrick was thinking. "You're going to adopt her," I said. It wasn't a question.

"Not really, but I'm going to help her. And I want you to be part of it."

Patrick was a much better judge of character than I, and he often saw some good in people that I completely missed. That must be the case now. We talked a few more seconds, until Skylar called me back with a loud, deliberate clearing of her voice. I returned to my apartment and looked at her in a whole new way.

Mom arrived a little after nine, laden down with groceries she had bought the day before. I expected that. What I didn't expect was the young girl who accompanied her. I knew instantly that it was the Adele I'd heard so much about yesterday. Her brown hair was pulled into a ponytail, high on her head the way young girls wear them, and she was dressed in jeans, stylishly faded and ripped, and a denim jacket that looked too expensive for a kid. A bright pink T-shirt under the jacket was perfectly matched by pink tennis shoes that also looked costly. Someone thought this kid was special. What struck me most, though, was the look on her face, which almost shouted at me, "I'm Adele, and I know you're glad to see me." Smug wasn't a strong enough word.

Mom, breathless from carrying groceries up three flights, said, "Henny, this is Adele. Adele, meet Henny." Then, still breathless, she added, "Adele didn't particularly want to go on the family boat ride, even though Ellie really wanted her to go."

Mom was still holding a bag of groceries when, to my amazement, Skylar came and wordlessly took the bag from her and set it on the kitchen table. And when Mom said, "Good morning, Skylar," she responded with "Mornin'" and I saw it again—that slight curve of the mouth.

Adele stared at Skylar in frank and rude curiosity and then turned away, dismissing Skylar with a slight shrug and returning to the subject of, what else—Adele. "Everybody wants my company today. I'm popular."

*And spoiled*, I added in my mind. What was wrong with Mom? She never would have tolerated such self-centeredness in me or my sisters. I decided Irene's danger had turned all of us into people we didn't understand.

Mom went on. "Her parents are going, but I think her mom was kind of relieved Adele didn't want to. She kept telling me Adele is a great cook and she could be a lot of help to me. We're glad she's here, aren't we, Henny, because now we get her company most of the day."

Adele looked at me quizzically, "Henny? What kind of a name is that? I never heard it before."

I couldn't resist. "That's why it's special," I said.

"Mom, remember tonight is Irene's book signing, and then Patrick's family wants to take us all to dinner. We'll probably go to a local Italian place."

She stopped in her tracks. "I guess I'll pass on the signing. I don't even want to know how to cook 'Fraunch.'" She caught Irene's intonation perfectly, and I couldn't help but laugh. "But we all like Italian food. That will be good."

"Patrick says we must invite Irene and Mr. Peterman."

"That's all right. I'll sit at the other end of the table . . . or the room. Whatever."

Well, now I knew that the spat of the other night over who taught me to cook was not going to blow over. In the face of everything else, it seemed a small thing.

Mom surprised me with the ingredients for Texas caviar. "I suspect Patrick has never eaten it," she said. "He'll like it." I knew he would, so while she bustled about unpacking and arranging things, I made Texas caviar. Within minutes Mom, ever efficient, had the potatoes boiling and the celery and onions out to be washed. I dunked the vegetables in cold water while Mom set up a workstation at the table with all the ingredients for dressing for the salad and barbecue sauce.

Mom turned to me. "Where's your colander?" I dug into the back of a cupboard and got it out, and she dumped the pinto beans in, rinsed them, and then put them in a pot of cold water. "Adele, come here, and I'll show you how to sort beans." With Adele standing dutifully beside her, she gave a lecture on broken beans and those that floated. I put on my special goggles and began chopping onions, a chore I despise. After she got Adele started, Mom began putting the ingredients for the barbecue sauce in a big pot she'd found in my shelves.

Our companionable silence lasted maybe all of three minutes. Adele began talking, though her talk was mostly disguised as questions. "Mrs. Foxglove didn't kill that other woman, did she? I just know she's not the kind to kill someone else. I am so excited to meet her." A pause and then, "How did you know that Mrs. Foxglove had drugs in her purse? I mean, how did you find them and how did you know what they were?" She was curious, no, make that nosey, about everything from where did I meet Patrick to when did I think the police would catch the bad men? Questions for which I had no answers. Eventually she gave up and apparently decided I was not worth bothering with. To my great relief, she turned her attention to Mom and cooking questions. But it struck me as odd that a child knew about murder and everything else that was going on. Did her parents not filter what they talked to her about?

My plan was to help Mom start the cooking—a lot of it, like sauce and beans, had to simmer and didn't require much work once it was started. Then I'd leave her in charge of the kitchen and run all those errands most brides would have done days, even weeks, earlier. Adele was just a slight complication—she could help Mom watch the pots. I hadn't figured Skylar into my planning.

No matter what happened between her and Patrick in the middle of the night, Skylar took her duties seriously. When I announced I was leaving, I expected she would insist on coming with me, and I was resigned to that. What I didn't expect was that she would announce that she could not leave an "older" woman (that's really what she said—lucky Mom didn't bash her with a pot of beans!) and a young child alone in my apartment nor could she let me go, even with Patrick for protection. I swore then and there that both Patrick and I were going to get gun licenses—I would send off today for that Firearm Owner's Permit application. But that didn't help today's problem.

I could exert my authority. After all, I wasn't under house arrest or anything—but that made me sound too much like Irene. At which thought, it occurred to me that I had no idea who replaced Linda Rutledge with Irene. I was curious but not curious enough to call and find out. Whoever it was had my sympathy.

Back to Skylar. If her presence was what Al Schmidt thought I needed, I'd be cooperative. I could do a lot of my so-called errands by phone. The one I couldn't do was a fitting for the wedding dress. Sigh. I surely wouldn't be the only bride who wore an ill-fitting gown on the biggest day of her life.

Because we had chosen a small, nontraditional wedding, I had never even considered a so-called gown. My dress would be somewhere between go-to-church and cocktails—a pale, pale beige street-length sheath with a V back and short cape sleeves, the color chosen to go with the Palmer House color scheme I was using. I saw a picture of the dress in black, found the exact shade of silk crepe I wanted, and took it all to a dressmaker, who said she could recreate the picture. I'd tried it on once and loved it, but it had needed some minor adjustments. Randy might take me tomorrow, but that was asking a lot of Mrs. Adams to adjust a dress in one day. I'd start my afternoon of calls with her.

And so I did, while Mom kept Adele busy and Skylar retreated into her shell. I wished fervently Patrick had not gone on the river trip and was instead home with us. He apparently softened or reassured Skylar somewhat.

Mrs. Adams was agreeable and comforting. She said she was quite confident of the nips and tucks she'd taken and was sure the dress would fit perfectly. I made a tentative appointment to be at her home Saturday morning

I called Elaine at 57th Street Books and confirmed that all was in order. She said they had several inquiries, and she expected a respectable number of guests. I kept to myself the thought that if they weren't plenty, one of us would have to deal with a hysterical, demanding diva.

Finally, reluctantly, I called Irene and burst right into what I needed to say so that she couldn't sidetrack me with a diatribe about who her current protector was. "Irene, I just want to remind you we need to be at the bookstore no later than four thirty." Okay, I moved it up a bit, because I didn't trust her. Even that proved too trusting.

"I'm not going," she said flatly.

"Not going?" The words echoed in my ear. "Excuse me, but you have to go. I busted my you-know-what to get this gig for you because you wanted to promote the cookbook I didn't know you'd written." It might well have been the harshest I have ever been with Madame.

"I will not appear in public with this foul creature," she said.

Foul creature? Visions of a human gargoyle took over my brain. "Pardon me?"

"This person they sent to protect me. He's rude, he's sloppily dressed, he has no manners. He does nothing to protect me. I am scared to leave my room."

It was a man. Did he sleep on Linda's rollaway? That thought almost made me laugh. But I sobered and realized, like Randy's substitute that night at the motel, he probably spent the night in the hallway. "What time did Linda say she would return?"

"She didn't say. I want to be rid of all of them. But if I can't go to the signing with just Raymond, I'm not going."

"I'm calling Detective Schmidt," I said, simply because no other bright ideas popped into my mind. Randy, were he here, would go with me to fetch her; Skylar would not hear of it. She would say that I, and I alone, was her responsibility.

Schmidt just sighed. "When did you say she's going back to France? I know she didn't kill that woman, but I can't just turn her loose. And if she's killed, my neck will really be on the chopping block."

I decided silence was my best choice. I waited.

Finally, after a long pause, he said, "I'll call Linda."

He called back within three minutes. "It seems Linda has developed a soft spot for your diva. She'll have her there by four thirty or shortly thereafter."

"What about Randy?" I asked.

"Don't push your luck," he said and hung up.

As it turned out, Skylar took me to the bookstore, but Randy met us there, and she departed with her usual lack of grace, though I saw her whisper something to Patrick, and he nodded in agreement. "I invited her to the rehearsal dinner," Patrick said proudly after she left. "There will be plenty of food, won't there?"

I was almost as ungracious as Skylar herself. "It's not the food I'm worried about."

He fixed me with a look, and I melted. "I'll be sweet, I promise. Besides, I don't think she'll show up." Someday I will learn to stop making predictions that turn out to be totally wrong.

With a grin, as he turned away, he kissed my forehead and said, "Being sweet might be hard."

When I asked Randy if there was any progress in finding out who the smugglers were, he shook his head. "Nothing."

"Nothing? How long does this go on?"

"Until it's over," he said.

Irene blew into the store at ten minutes before five, greeted me with a warm embrace, was gracious and enthusiastic to Elaine. Anybody who watched her would wonder what kind of a witch I was to have said such unkind things about her. Sometimes I wondered myself.

Tonight, she wore yet another suit in that faux Chanel style, with the boxy jacket, this one in a bright coral that flattered her complexion and was perfectly matched by the lipstick she wore. Her hair was still drawn back into a chignon, but she had artfully pulled a few strands loose so that they framed her face. Most of all her blue eyes sparkled with enthusiasm. She was the center of attention, the star she always wanted to be.

Patrick arrived, shepherding everyone in my family except Mom, promptly at five o'clock. Their arrival gave the impression of a small crowd, which bolstered Irene's spirits. I noticed that my sisters wore tailored slacks, and I wanted to tell them this was not the kind of place where they needed to bother. The fashionably torn jeans they usually wore would have been fine. Ray Peterman arrived shortly thereafter, fussing over Irene with a courtly bow. My sisters each bought a book, and Irene signed them with a flourish. And then bit by bit real customers stopped by. A few just chatted but several bought a book, and Irene was ever the gracious diva. She was in her element, and I felt I could stop holding my breath. Linda studied every person who approached Irene, no matter how innocent they looked, and I knew Randy was at the front of the store, monitoring who came in.

Patrick put a loving arm around me and whispered in my ear, "Henny, you worry too much."

Little did he know.

# Chapter Thirteen

The party—and the diva—were wearing down. It was about six thirty, another half hour to go. Suddenly one of those men who commands the whole room strode back to the area where Irene was sitting, closely followed by a suspicious Randy. Linda quickly clutched her purse which, I knew, held a handgun.

The man was neither young nor old, not exactly handsome but, as I said, commanding. He had dark hair, graying at the temples, and he was clean-shaven, which revealed irregular facial features—deep-set eyes with bushy eyebrows, a nose a bit too big that looked like it had once been broken, and a full mouth that was slightly off-center. But he had the one feature I always look for—a strong chin.

Somehow the room seemed to freeze as everyone stopped talking and stared at him. It didn't faze him at all, and he walked deliberately toward Irene. It was a minute before she looked up, but when she did her face was transformed. Her face turned pale, her mouth slightly open as though she wanted to speak and couldn't. She was no longer the center of attention—someone had robbed her of that, and she knew it, but she didn't look regretful. Finally, she spoke.

"Chance!"

With one word, she cleared up a whole lot of the mystery. Of course, it was Chance. But why had he come here? Was he personally going to try to talk her into giving him the cocaine? Smart as he was, didn't he realize she didn't have it anymore? I am not one to automatically distrust a good-looking man—I was marrying Patrick, wasn't I?—but I'd heard too much, the good and the bad, about Chance Charpentier to be anything but suspicious.

He, however, seemed perfectly at ease and in command of the situation. With one fluid movement, he was in front of her, bowing over the hand she held out to him. After a quick kiss, he raised his eyes to meet hers and said, loud enough for all of us to hear, "Mon amour Irene, I came as quickly as I could."

She stammered and stared and managed to ask, "How did you know there was … ah, difficulty?"

He straightened and shrugged casually. "Gabrielle. She spoke with a detective named Schmidt."

Irene obviously didn't know that and waited cautiously for what he would say next.

"My plane is always on standby, with a packed suitcase. I was airborne within an hour of Gabrielle's call." Then he added, casually, "She is doing well with the café. Our daughter"—did he emphasize that link that tied them to each other? — "is making us proud."

"Merci," Irene murmured.

I marveled at a lifestyle I could not even imagine. A private plane always ready to go, with a packed suitcase. Was his business often that urgent, or was he an impulsive traveler, giving in to whims to be somewhere other than where he was? I suppose his explanation about his plane only fueled my dislike. I may not have distrusted handsome men, but like many Americans, even Texans, I had that instant distrust of the very wealthy. After all, how could he have honestly accumulated such wealth? No, it had to be tainted money.

Patrick, as always, brought me back to earth. An arm around my shoulders, he whispered, "Don't rush to judgment, Henny. Let's just listen." And listen I did—and watch.

Looking at the scene from the sidelines, I turned my attention to Ray Peterman. The expression on his face had gone from shock to dismay, and he, too, was pale. But he recovered quickly. In the awkward pause that followed, Peterman stepped forward, his hand outstretched, and said, almost too heartily, "Monsieur Charpentier,

Ray Peterman. Irene has spoken of you so often. It is an unexpected pleasure to meet you." Did the word "unexpected" have an edge to it?

Charpentier looked a lot happier about this meeting than Peterman. "The hotel man?" he asked in a rhetorical question. "My father talked of you and your many kindnesses to him. I am forever at your service, monsieur." He didn't settle for a handshake but went for a full embrace with much clapping of his hand on Ray's back. Finally, he straightened and said solemnly, "But now, we must talk about how we can save Irene, oui?"

*I already did that once,* I thought, sharing my thought with Patrick through a squeeze of the hand I held. He squeezed back, and I knew he understood. We had saved her, but we were about to be eclipsed by this flashy Frenchie.

The room, which had suddenly lapsed into frozen silence, came slowly to life again as people began to whisper among themselves, no doubt speculating on the relationship between Madame, Peterman, and Chance. There were perhaps fifteen people, either waiting for a chance to approach Irene or browsing in nearby shelves. Those who were browsing were immediately drawn into the drama playing out before them.

Slowly one brave soul, a woman who appeared to be about Irene's age but quite a bit less stylishly dressed, approached Irene's table. She took a book off the stack, and held it out, wordlessly, for a signature. Perhaps the woman forgot momentarily that Irene spoke English and was undone by the thought of French. Irene was back to her diva role, graciously asking how she should sign it.

"To Hannah," the woman said. "Could you write it in French?"

That stymied even Irene momentarily, and, worried as I was, I had to stifle a laugh.

Irene bent to the task, but when she looked up, Chance took the book, looked at Hannah, with her backpack slung over one shoulder, and asked, in his most charming manner, "May I?"

When she nodded, he bent and wrote something long enough to be a sentence or two, obviously in French. Smiling he handed it back to her and translated, "May you find health and happiness in these recipes."

Hannah grinned and began digging in her backpack, apparently for money to pay for the book. Gradually others followed her lead, stepping out of the crowd to buy a book. We had thought Irene had sold all she would, but as it turned out she sold out of both cartons.

Elaine sidled up to me. "I sure wish I knew this whole story," she said. "Did you plan this as a sales gimmick? If so, I'm taking lessons from you."

Next to me, Patrick snorted, a most uncivilized sound, and I could barely keep a straight face as I said, "I only wish. He's supposed to be in France. I can guarantee Irene didn't even have a clue he was coming. I can't tell you the whole story, but it puts her in a difficult spot. Me, too."

"I'll buy supper," she offered, only half joking, but I told her we had dinner plans.

Irene, now standing behind the table, flanked by both her apparent suitors, waved for Patrick and me to approach. It wasn't just a wave—it was a command. I felt like we were approaching royalty.

"My dear Henrietta," she said and then, expansively, "and Patrick, of course, you must meet Gabrielle's father, Chance Charpentier."

As he bowed over my hand, I thought that was an odd way to describe him—not that I would have had her say "My former lover" or "My benefactor," or anything like that, but she could maybe have said, "My friend."

He turned to Patrick with a hearty, "And you are the groom? Are you sure about this, young man?"

Quickly offering his hand to avoid an embrace, Patrick said, "Yes, sir. I am quite sure." As if to emphasize he moved a bit closer to me and put a possessive arm around my waist.

"Good, because I am looking forward to attending the wedding," he said heartily.

My first thought was, "We're gathering quite a crowd, and the cost is going up," quickly followed by a more devastating thought, "If there is a wedding."

Randy and Linda stood together off to one side. I could tell they were watching Chance Charpentier closely, though they were unobtrusive about it. Casually dressed, they simply looked like a married couple come to buy a French cookbook. Unless you knew, as I did, to look for that telltale bulge under Randy's sport jacket or the sleeve in Linda's purse from which she could draw a handgun with lightning speed.

I sent them a weak grin, which they both ignored. They really acted like they were enjoying each other's company, and though I knew it was an act, I began to wonder if Linda had a husband or a boyfriend.

Patrick's whisper brought me sharply back to the present problem. "What are we going to do?" he asked.

"About what?" My teeth were clenched.

"Everything," he replied, "but right now I had my parents in mind."

I pulled him aside, so that we were well away from the crowd. Totally ignoring his worry about his parents, I said, "We have to see what happens. Chance knows she's a so-called person of interest in a murder. And obviously he knows about the wedding. What we don't know is what he knows about the drugs." I glanced in Irene's direction and saw Chance standing confidently in front of the table—blocking sales—and Ray hovering nervously behind her. Whether or not he was nervous about competition in the romance department was the least of my problems. More immediate was to find out why Chance had come from France—it would have to be something important. Irene or drugs? I was betting on the latter. In fact, I bet he knew the dead woman, Simone Guillaume.

Such weighty questions were not what Patrick wanted to talk about. "My parents," he repeated, his voice almost a whine. So unlike him. When I looked straight at him, he said, "They will be waiting for us at Piccolo Mondo." He looked distinctly unhappy. "I hate to cater to them, but well, Mom . . ." His voice trailed off, but I got the picture. "She doesn't like to be kept waiting."

"You'll have to tell them we're a bit delayed . . . and that our party is growing every minute." I counted on my fingers: five of my family, including me, Patrick and his parents, Randy, Linda, Irene, Ray, and now Chance. "Patrick!" I almost spit his name out. "That's thirteen! It's bad luck."

His old, familiar grin came back. "Why, Henny, who would have thought you were superstitious!" He gave me a quick kiss and said, "Hurry everyone along as best you can."

Little did I suspect what would happen before I saw him again.

I began with my dad. "Will you take the girls, go get Mom, and meet us at Piccolo Mondo? I can draw you a quick map. It's easy, and not too far from your hotel."

Dad agreed but reminded me that Mom was still babysitting Adele, the spoiled brat. "Her folks wanted a romantic dinner for two, and your mom was glad to help out. I just didn't think it through that it would be a problem with our dinner. Besides," he added with a grin, "your mom is enjoying having a little girl for a while, even if it's not her own daughter."

Sigh. At least Adele would make fourteen at the table and move us beyond unlucky thirteen. I bit my tongue to keep from saying what I thought of that particular little girl. But I did think about adding yet another mouth to the table when Patrick's parents were hosting. "Dad, you'll just have to be sure to pick up the check for our family . . . and Adele."

"I can do that. No problem. Don't worry, sweetie. We'll see you shortly at dinner. I'm looking forward to some really good lasagna."

Once they were off, I approached Irene, figuring it was best to start with the wild card. "Irene, we need to be leaving for the restaurant."

"Oh, of course. To meet Patrick's parents, such dear people they must be to have such a son, non? We are going to the Palmer House?"

"No, a restaurant here in Hyde Park called Piccolo Mondo. You'll like it." I crossed my fingers because I knew that was a little white lie. She was generally scornful of Italian, as she was of almost any cuisine that was not French.

Predictably, she drew back in horror. "Italian? I cannot do it." Her face was set in stone, her tone emphatic.

It was Chance who came to my rescue, smiling affectionately at Irene. "My dear, I can help you order, and you will love it. Perhaps they will have the scallops Grenobloise, eh?"

Irene smiled benevolently at him, and I fought back an urge to comment on how quickly she went from sour to sweet.

Ray was still hovering nervously at her elbow. "Irene, my dear, don't you want to powder your nose before we go? I'll go get the car, and perhaps Monsieur Charpentier will be kind enough to ride with us."

"No need for that, Ray. I have a chauffeur waiting. You can ride with us, and we'll bring you back later to get your car." His inclusion of Ray banished one of my fears. I doubted Chance realized that Linda went everywhere Irene did, and I had already spun a terrible tale in my mind wherein he kidnapped Irene and—what? Held her hostage for the drugs? He was too charming, too open—I suspected him of the darkest things.

Irene, meanwhile, fussed and said, "Of course, I must repair to the ladies' room." As Linda started after her, she said archly, "No need for you, Ms. Rutledge. I can take care of my business myself."

"No, ma'am," Linda said with equal determination. "I am going with you."

I remembered that Elaine, showing me around the first day I visited about the signing, had showed me the ladies' room. It—and the men's room—was down a small hallway with a door at the end, a light over it flashing a red sign, "Emergency exit only." The only other door was to a locked supply room.

"The exit door is always locked," Elaine had explained, "and a loud alarm goes off if anybody opens it."

I thought at the time it was a pretty secure arrangement, but still Linda was smart to go with Madame.

Chance looked puzzled, and I explained, "Undercover police. Protection for Irene until that murder is solved, and the drug ring participants are arrested." That, I thought, should make him recalculate his plans, but he looked unfazed.

Chance simply nodded his head and murmured, "Good. That relieves me a bit. I came to Chicago because of my great concern for Irene."

Likely, I thought.

While we waited for Irene to powder her nose and take care of whatever other business, I had a brief conference with Elaine. She would total up sales, take the store's forty percent—Irene would gasp at that, I knew, but I also knew it was the bookstore standard—and she would have the balance hand-delivered to Irene at the Palmer House.

"I am very pleased," she said, "and so grateful that you brought this event to us." Then in an undertone, "But I still want to know the story about the Frenchman. Can we have a drink next week?"

Next week, in my mind, was a million miles off. "Sure," I said. "I'd like that."

The minutes crept by, and Irene did not appear. Chance, that self-composed man, began to pace. Randy eyed the hall to the restrooms with distrust. I had to clench my fists to keep from biting my nails. Even Elaine looked nervous and managed to say, "Our ladies' room is not comfortable enough to linger in."

Randy finally sidled over to me and said, "Would you go check on them? I'll be right behind you."

Thinking this was ridiculous and probably another of Irene's attention-getting ploys, I strode down the short hall and with a firm gesture pushed open the door. And then I screamed bloody murder—and screamed and screamed.

Irene was not there, Linda lay sprawled on the floor, either unconscious or dead, I wasn't sure which, and the room showed signs of a struggle—a trash can overturned, the chair by a dressing table upended, rags on the floor.

Randy knocked me aside as he rushed in, and I promptly fainted.

# Chapter Fourteen

I awoke, in confusion and then terror, to find Chance Charpentier's face inches from mine. I was flat on my back in the hallway outside the bookstore's ladies' room and only vaguely aware of people and strained voices around me. My first coherent thought was insane: he was going to strangle me. With a sudden jerk, I tried to sit up, only to be pushed back down to the floor with strong hands.

"No, chérie, take your time. Lie there a minute and collect yourself." His voice was gentle, especially for a drug lord. Maybe he was only going to kidnap me and take me to Irene. "Irene?" I asked.

He shook his head. "We don't know anything."

The scene was slowly coming back to me. "How long have I been here?"

"Just a couple of minutes. You fainted. A shock your mind didn't want to deal with."

*So now he's a psychiatrist?* A new memory crept it: Linda lying motionless on the floor. "Linda?"

"She will be fine. There was a rag soaked in chloroform next to her. They—whoever they are—probably used it on Irene too." His slight chuckle was ironic. "How else would they get her out of here quietly?"

The door. The exit door Elaine had so carefully explained to me was safe. Someone must have disabled the alarm, and whoever took Irene came in and out that way. Could someone in the signing crowd have turned off the alarm? I stared at Chance Charpentier for a long time, but if he were guilty, he hid it well.

I tried again to sit up and this time he helped me, supporting my back with one arm. And when I tried to stand, he steadied me. I was wobbly but okay. Once on my feet, I knew that I needed Patrick—immediately. I needed him to steady my world.

Chance was ahead of me. "You must call that fiancé of yours and tell him what happened."

"He's having dinner with his parents and my family. I . . . I have never met the parents."

He shook his head and another small, ironic smile crept across his face. "Now is not a good time, no?"

"What is he going to tell them?" I hesitated and then plunged on. "We can't have a wedding without Irene!" Did I hear my own words? Did I know how far I'd come from resenting that she flown across the ocean to ruin my wedding to declaring I couldn't get married without her? Chance knew none of that, fortunately.

He led me to the table where Irene had signed, sat me down, and said he'd be right back with coffee. I wanted wine but agreed that black coffee would be good. What seemed like an army of police officers swarmed around me, but they gave me wide berth, and I ignored them. While Chance was gone, I hit one for Patrick on my phone and realized that my hands were shaking so that I could barely hold the phone. I didn't dare use speaker, and I warned Patrick not to.

He sounded out of sorts. "Where are you? We are all hungry."

That did it! I burst into tears, loud sobs. Chance quietly put my coffee in front of me and took the phone. Speaking rapidly in his French-tinged English he told Patrick what had happened. "Oui, you must make some excuse . . . No, I don't think you should tell them the whole story yet." Satisfied, he ended the call and said, "He'll be right here. Don't move."

*Why was I in the hands of the man who I knew to be at the least a cad and at the worst probably a drug dealer? Where was all that independence I bragged about? Once Patrick gets here, I'll be back to myself.*

But I wasn't. Al Schmidt, who now seemed like a savior to me, arrived before Patrick. Before he even came back to the signing area, he loudly—I could hear him plainly—closed the store, kicking out customers and staff alike, except for a couple of managers who he grudgingly allowed to stay. I heard him proclaim "It's a crime scene!" more than once. I was sure Elaine was among those sent home, so I couldn't ask about the door. Surely Schmidt would figure it out.

Al Schmidt had much more on his mind than comforting me when he finally came to the back of the store. He gave me an unprecedent hug, murmured, "I'll be back," and disappeared down that hallway. I was beginning to have the feeling that people who went into that blank space might never return.

But then there came Linda, not from the hallway but from the front of the store, walking slowly and leaning on a uniformed medic. The medic, a woman, seated her at the table, but when I asked Linda how she was, she looked confused, as though she were unsure who I was. "My head is pounding," she said. "They gave me something, but it's not working yet. I'm not sure what happened."

I murmured appropriate sympathies, but I wasn't about to be the one to tell her that she'd failed in her one duty: saving Irene from danger. I was beginning to account for everyone: Irene was missing, Patrick was on his way to me, our families were at Piccolo Mondo, enjoying, I hoped, a hearty lasagna or spaghetti with meatballs, Linda was next to me, Randy must be in the ladies' room with some of those officers, and Chance—he was everywhere, wringing his hands, worrying about Irene and me and Linda, and saying he must call Gabrielle. I didn't want him to do that, but something else bothered me until it worked its way to the front of my brain: Ray Peterman. Where was he?

The next time Chance walked by the table, I reached out and grabbed his hand. "Ray? Where is he?"

He looked around, as though looking for him. "I don't know. He was here . . . Let me check." With a mission in mind, Chance seemed more in control. He headed down that hallway, presumably to look for Ray in either of the restrooms. I had that sinking feeling of watching another person disappear down there.

But Chance was promptly back. "It is strange," he said very carefully. "No one saw him leave, but he is clearly not here. He must have slipped out during the confusion."

*Strange. You'd think he'd be so anxious about Irene that he'd be hovering. Was his health okay? Was this all too much for him? If so, I could sympathize.*

Finally, Patrick burst into the signing area, with a loud cry of "Henny!" and arms outspread. I stood up and walked into his embrace, feeling my knees go weak again now that he was there. He stroked my hair and rubbed my back and murmured sweet nothings in my ear.

Eventually, I raised a tear-stained face, looked at him, and said, "Patrick, I can't marry you."

Despite all that had happened, Patrick tossed his head back and roared with laughter.

Hurt, I gave him my best puzzled look.

"Oh, Henny," he said when he could finally speak again, "I am so glad you're still you."

I never did get to explain that I knew now for sure that the wedding of my dreams to the man of my dreams was not happening in two days.

About nine o'clock, Schmidt cleared the store of all but what he called essential personnel. That meant Patrick and me and Chance. To me, the detective said, "You can go to my headquarters. I'll be there shortly. It'll be the command station, where I can direct things and keep track. But I want to talk to you, just haven't had time."

Patrick and I left in his car, and I presumed Chance and his chauffeur would follow. But they never showed up at the station. It was a momentary worry, but I was busy checking on my family, and Patrick on his. They were all worried, scared, confused, and there was little we could do to comfort them.

My parents—well, really my sisters—still had Adele. "Looks like we'll put her to sleep in the girls' room, that cot you slept on," Dad said over the phone. "Her parents said they ran into some old friends, and would we mind if they stayed out late. What could we say?"

An unladylike retort went through my mind, but I wouldn't say it to my father. Still, the last thing we needed right now was an eight-year-old with flighty parents. "You're good to take care of her" was the best I could manage. "I'll let you know if anything happens."

"Good. We're all worried about Irene . . . and you."

Listening in on Patrick's conversation, I gathered his parents—or at least his mother—was not only confused but also unsure of the wedding.

"Mom, let's not go over that again. No, nothing's going to change."

Didn't take a rocket scientist to figure out what that was about. No wonder in all the long year we'd been courting, he'd never taken me to Winnetka to meet them.

It was close to midnight before Schmidt called us into his stuffy, smoke-filled office. I fidgeted in my uncomfortable chair, wondering what I could possibly add to what he already knew.

"I want to talk about who was there when Mrs. Foxglove actually went missing." He looked at Patrick. "You had already left?"

"Yessir."

Then, to me, "And your family had gone?"

I nodded. "Ray Peterman was there—the Palmer House historian." As if he didn't know. "And Chance Charpentier. Randy and Linda."

"Otherwise just customers? No one else you knew?" He didn't even wait for me to go on. "One of the customers could have disabled the alarm and opened the door. I've asked the manager to pull all the tickets, so we can check charge cards and checks for name and address. Only ones that would slip by us are customers who paid cash. Or didn't buy anything. We're not just talking about the people who came for the cookbook. Anybody in the store."

Sounded thorough to me.

"But I'm more concerned about the ones you knew, not counting Randy and Linda. She, by the way, is fine and stands ready to do whatever she can to help. What about Mr. Peterman?"

"He's harmless," I said with assurance. "He's smitten with Irene, and he's just a kind old man. In fact, I thought he looked unwell tonight. He was paler than usual and not quite as self-confident, as though he were anxious. I know his sister has been ill, so maybe she has taken a turn for the worse and he felt he should be with her, but he also wanted to be here for Irene. He left during the commotion when we couldn't find Irene."

Schmidt was scribbling on a legal pad with a stubby pencil while I talked. "Okay, he doesn't sound suspicious, but you never know. We'll check him out, but he's low on the list. We are checking hospitals right now, also cab companies. Wish there was some way to check Uber drivers but that's like trying to catch waves in Lake Michigan."

He hadn't gotten to the one person I still thought needed investigating. "Chance Charpentier left when we did, and I thought he was coming here. Do you know where he went?"

Patrick gave me one of his stern looks and shook his head ever so slightly. I knew he thought I was judging Chance unfairly, and he hadn't even seen how kind the man had been to me when I fainted. But I'd told him about it. And now, suspecting him made me feel a bit guilty.

"Nope, and I haven't met him or talked to him. He's not at the Palmer House, I can tell you that. We've been over the roster of guests, done a sweep of the hotel. She's not there. I'll stake my career on that."

"Does it concern you where Chance is? He's the mystery figure to me," I said, earning another frown from Patrick.

"We're checking his background in France," Schmidt explained. "May turn up friends or relatives here that he's gone to stay with. I can't see him coming all the way here to kidnap her."

"He would if he had a stake in that cocaine," I suggested.

He shook his head. "Charpentier is too wealthy and too prominent to mess with that."

His determination not to consider Chance Charpentier bothered me—a lot.

He saw it in my face. "We'll check with the French consulate. I know there are French groups in Chicago, one on the North Shore."

"Maybe he has a network." I couldn't stop myself. In my mind, Schmidt was full of things he was going to look into, sort of casually, sometime in the future. I wanted answers now. I . . . truth is, I wanted Irene back. And I wanted to marry Patrick—in two days! To keep myself from crying, I grabbed his hand.

"As in a new French underground, Henny?" Schmidt shook his head. "I think you are letting your imagination run away with you."

It was the most impatient the detective had ever been with me, and between Gabrielle's kidnapping and now Irene missing, he'd had plenty of opportunity. I stayed quiet, clutching Patrick's hand.

Before we knew it, we were back in that waiting room, sitting on unforgiving plastic furniture, sipping cold, bitter coffee. "You hungry?" Patrick asked. "You eat anything all evening?"

I shook my head. "No. You?"

"I don't think I can eat. I had just ordered chicken scallopini and roasted artichokes."

"Yum." Any other time that selection would have me salivating, but not now.

"We can order in some hamburgers."

"Not for me. You?" I couldn't stifle a yawn.

"No," he said. "Pretty soon it will be breakfast time. Put your head on my shoulder and try to sleep."

"I couldn't."

So we sat, holding hands, watching an old round wall clock that ticked ever so slowly and made me think of my grade school classroom.

We spent a long miserable night in Schmidt's police station. I didn't want to go home and sit by the phone, and Randy didn't like that idea anyway. He was pulled from protecting me to, as he said, "work the kidnapping"—I guess they figured if the bad guys had Irene, they wouldn't take me too. I'm sure the reassignment made Randy happy, but I thought I'd been abandoned again.

# Chapter Fifteen

Although I swore I could not sleep for worrying, I finally curled up with my head in Patrick's lap and lay there, uncomfortable and wide awake. He, poor thing, kept an arm about me, threw back his head, and began to snore softly. He would have a stiff neck when he awoke. Somehow, without realizing it, I finally drifted off.

And that's how Schmidt found us, a little before five in the morning. I wasn't even aware that he was speaking until Patrick gently shook me awake. I had slept soundly but not well, my sleep filled with terrifying dreams of Irene being held prisoner, of Adele taunting her—how did Adele end up in my dream? When Patrick shook me, I was almost grateful to be wakened. I scrambled upright and demanded "What's happening?" in way too loud a voice.

Speaking more softly, the detective said, "There's been a break of sorts, though I don't know how far ahead it puts us. And it happened by coincidence. We got a call to do a wellness check on a condo on North Lincoln. Lady saw unusual activity at her neighbor's place around three o'clock—don't ask me why she was spying on her neighbor at that hour, but she was. Saw people go in and out, but an old man lives there alone."

My heart sank. I thought I knew where this was going, and I didn't like it. My mind's eye saw Ray Peterman, looking so nervous at the signing.

"The responding officer thought it was probably a dead end, but we check out all such calls. She didn't get any response when she knocked, rang the doorbell, even called out loud. So she forced entry and found an elderly man on the floor unconscious." He nodded as if agreeing with what we had left unspoken. "Your friend, Peterman. Looks like someone hit him in the head. Pretty hard."

"But he's alive?" Patrick asked, with more common sense than I could muster.

"Yeah. He came around. Could talk a bit, though he seemed confused. Officer called for an ambulance, and they transported him."

He was putting all the wrong parts of the story first. "What did he say? Was Irene there?" My impatience showed.

"She was before we got there. A couple named Parker, North—honest, that's his first name—and Emily snatched her from the signing." He took a deep breath. "We know they are the couple who are staying at the Lake Shore Hotel where your folks are. We don't know, though, how they connected your family to you and ended up at the motel. But they're the ones who 'just happened' to meet your family at the museum and then went on the river cruise with them. They blackmailed Peterman into unlocking that rear door and disarming the alarm by threatening his sister. Did you say she's sick or something?"

I nodded. "In Peoria, not here."

"Still vulnerable, apparently. Told him they had someone watching her place. We've called Peoria, asked for a wellness check on her. They'll keep someone with her for a bit till we get this all sorted out."

I didn't give a fig about Ray's sister—well, that was unkind. I did care, but I cared a whole lot more about Irene. It all came together—the Parkers' eagerness to know all the details of our weekend, their pretend awe at Irene's celebrity status, even why Adele didn't go on the river trip. I told Schmidt all of it, right down to what a brat Adele was. "But surely they didn't plan all this from France. Do they know Chance? Why do they want Irene?"

"We have nothing to link them to Mr. Charpentier. I assume, though, they somehow heard about the drugs and wanted to be part of the deal—or even edge out whoever else. I guess maybe they believe she's still got the stuff." He gave me a long look, as though assessing my strength.

"Adele is part of all this!" What kind of people involve an eight-year-old child? No wonder she had so many questions about murder.

"Adele is the child, I presume. Right now, we don't know where Adele is. We'll get Family Services involved when we find her, but apparently, she was not with her parents."

My imagination sprang to work. "She's with my family. Asleep in my sisters' room. But what if she's not even their child?"

"You met her?" he asked gruffly. "She seem abused, frightened?"

I thought back to—was it only yesterday morning? "No, as I told you, she was, if anything, overindulged. A spoiled brat."

"Then she's theirs," he concluded. "Call your folks. Tell them a unit will be there shortly. I need a court order to take charge of the minor, but we can provide security until we see what the Parkers are going to do. Don't alarm your folks."

And how was I supposed to make that call without alarming them? And what if the Parkers came for their child before the police arrived? A vision of slaughter rose unbidden, until I batted it down and told myself to be sensible.

Patrick saw the concern—okay, fright—on my face. "Want me to call?"

I shook my head. "No, I'll do it." Even as I punched in number four for Dad on my phone, I heard Schmidt talking into his shoulder mic, requesting a team to the Lake Shore Hotel and giving them sketchy details of what they were to do.

My call immediately alarmed my mom and dad, as I knew it would. Like any good parents, they knew a five o'clock in the morning call from a child, even a grown daughter, was not good news. Dad's voice was fuzzy for maybe a nanosecond, but then with real alarm, he said, "Henny? Are you all right?"

"I'm fine, but there's a problem, and I need you to expect police at your door any minute. They'll want Adele. It's a long story, and I'll share it later today, but her parents are not who or what you think they are. You may have to turn Adele over to Family Services or something like that."

I could hear him turn and whisper to Mom, who let out a shriek. "We won't surrender that child to anyone without authority."

Time to be patient. "They have authority, Mom. The police won't take her without a court order, but there is good reason to believe that Adele is in danger." I took a deep breath. "And you could be too."

Mom wasn't buying it. "Adele is safe here with us."

I took a deep breath. "No, Mom, she's not. And as long as you have her, you and Dad and my sisters are not safe." I handed Patrick my phone, and said to Schmidt, "We need to be there. Right now. They're upset." I thought that was a mild word to use for it.

Within what seemed only seconds, we were in Schmidt's car, me in the passenger seat and Patrick in back, leaning forward to hold my hand as we roared south toward the hotel. Schmidt had one of those portable cherry things that he slapped on top of the car and turned on, so we flew with lights blazing and a siren blaring. I wondered if the siren would warn the Parkers. Warn them of what? And if they showed up to get Adele, they surely wouldn't bring Irene with them. My mind went in circles. If they hadn't dumped Irene—I refused to say Irene's body even to myself—maybe they wouldn't come for Adele. Best-case scenario in my mind, but it didn't get us any closer to Irene.

Schmidt dampened the siren and turned off the light as we pulled into the hotel parking lot. "No use waking all the guests," he said. Two police cruisers were angled in front of the main entrance, but there was no sign of their occupants. It was nearly six now, and darkness had turned into daylight since Schmidt woke us. A breeze off the lake would have felt welcome any other time, but now it just chilled me.

I ran through the lobby, with the desk clerk staring at me and raising a futile hand as though to stop me. I was oblivious, until later, of my wrinkled dress with a coffee stain on it. Nor did it dawn on me that I was hungry. Patrick was right behind me, but Schmidt stopped to talk to the puzzled desk clerk.

I arrived at Mom and Dad's room breathless and frantic, only to find a police officer standing smack in front of the door.

"No admittance," he said without any expression.

"My parents are in there!" I shouted.

Patrick put a restraining hand on my shoulder. "Shhh. You'll wake everyone, and we don't need a crowd of spectators. Detective Schmidt will be here any second now."

Furious, I started to turn on him, until I saw the love and fright in his eyes. His hand moved from my shoulder as he wrapped his arms around me and whispered, "It's gonna be all right, Henny. Honest, it is."

Schmidt arrived at that moment. All it took was one nod from him, and the officer opened the door and moved aside. I flew into the room and ended up in a bear hug from Dad, barely aware that a second officer was discreetly leaving the room. Only later did I realize that officer was Randy.

"I was so scared," I sobbed, looking around to see my sisters and Adele sitting on one of the beds, still in their pajamas, and Mom right next to Dad, reaching to be part of the hug.

"Shhh. It's okay," Dad said, smoothing my wild, unruly hair back like he used to when I was little. "Let's all sit down."

My knees were suddenly so weak I thought I'd sink to the floor. Dad guided me to the other bed, and Patrick slid in next to me, a comforting arm about my shoulders.

"We've asked Adele if she knows where her parents are," Dad said, "but she's no help."

Schmidt's next action left me open-mouthed with surprise. He went to Adele and got down on one knee. Taking her hand gently in his, he said, "Honey, we'll find your folks, and you'll be well taken care of until we do."

She was not moved by his kindness. "My parents don't want to be found," she said. "They'll come for me eventually, but they said they had work to do. For several days. But they always come for me." She was more than a bit defiant.

Schmidt nodded as though that were perfectly understandable and stood, patting Adele's head as he walked away.

"Please don't pat my head," she said crisply. "I am not a child."

It wasn't enough we were worried about Irene, but we also had to put up with this brat! Her statement of "several days" gave me hope they weren't planning to kill Irene, but then I wondered why there hadn't been a ransom demand of some kind. Patrick read my mind and shook his head slightly, his way of telling me now was not the time to bring that up.

"Folks," Schmidt said, standing back so he could address all of us, "we're going to ask you to stay here, under guard, for a while till we get this solved and hopefully get Mrs. Foxglove back in good shape. If you're hungry, I'll be glad to order in food from the hotel's coffee shop." He nodded to Patrick. "Would you look in that bedside drawer for a room service menu?"

And boom! Just like that I was ravenous. So, apparently, was my family. We ordered the works—eggs and bacon and sausage and potatoes and fruit. Only Adele held out for a Belgian waffle, and I hoped she didn't get a sugar high from it.

While we waited for breakfast to arrive, Patrick and Schmidt both excused themselves to make phone calls. Patrick came back rather swiftly, with a disappointed look on his face. "Mom says since the wedding is cancelled, they'll go back to Winnetka today." He said it softly, hoping no one else would hear, but I saw Mom's eagle eye fixed on him.

The wedding! How could I banish it from my mind? It hadn't once crossed my mind since the signing party. And tonight was the no-rehearsal rehearsal dinner at Promontory Point. The food was all ready, and I simply cannot bear to waste food. Plus, it would soon be too late to cancel the Palmer House arrangements. I took a deep breath, looked at Patrick, whose expression had turned hopeful, and whispered, "Tell them not to be in a hurry. There will be a wedding."

He gave me a huge, long kiss—in front of everyone—and hurried back into the hall. My sisters clapped their approval.

Almost a week ago, I thought Irene would ruin my wedding. Now it looked like, through no fault of her own, she was about to, but only if I let it be ruined. I wasn't going to do that, even if we had to marry with a platoon of police surrounding us.

Schmidt had nothing to announce when he came back, but said he still had to insist we all stay in this one room for security's sake.

"It's okay," Ellie said, "we have games and cards. We can amuse ourselves." Then she added, "But I'd like to be out by supper. I'm really looking forward to that barbecue. We need some good Texas food."

Breakfast arrived, and we ate until we could eat no more and then set the trays out in the hall for pickup as Randy, who had re-entered the room, suggested. I took the last tray, and Randy held the door open for me. The officer had stepped aside, and I wasn't paying attention. Neither, apparently, was Randy, because Adele, in a sudden bolt of action, ran out the door and headed toward the exit. Almost before we could react, she was out the door at the end of the hallway, setting off a wailing alarm, and into the parking lot. Randy broke into a sprint after her. I expected the officer at the door to follow, but he stayed at his post, explaining he had to be sure it wasn't a trick to leave us without protection. Dad went back into the room and brought the guy a straight chair.

At first, I was sure Randy would be right back, dragging an obstinate—and perhaps kicking—Adele. But that didn't happen. My uneasiness grew intense, and when Patrick joined me in the hall, I gripped his hand so tightly he uttered a soft, "Ouch!" My eyes were fixed on the door.

Almost simultaneously, I heard the roar of a car engine and shots—no, not a car backfiring. These were shots, three of them. I would have run down the hall to that door if Patrick hadn't kept a firm grip on me and issued a stern, "Wait!"

It was only a few seconds before Randy came through the door, now walking slowly, talking on the mic he always had clipped to the front of his shirt and clutching his left arm with his right hand. Patrick let go of me, and we both ran to him.

He turned away, signaling that he wanted to finish his call, but I saw blood seeping down his arm and whispered to Patrick to go grab a towel.

"Ford Explorer, white, probably a year or two old, definitely not new. Big dent on right rear." The other person apparently said something, and Randy replied, "Couldn't tell, but I don't think so. They'd obviously practiced this little trick, taught the kid to jump into a moving car. Once she was clinging to the handle, whoever was driving gunned it, and somebody fired at me." Another pause. "Three shots. Yeah, one grazed my arm. I'm okay. No, not going to the hospital. Okay, thanks." He hung up and faced me.

"Take your shirt off," I commanded.

"Pardon me?"

"Your arm is bleeding. We have to do something, treat it somehow."

"Could we do it in the room and not out here in the hall? Please?" He almost had a grin, and I wanted to slap him. I was frantic and he was making jokes.

Patrick walked up with a wet towel—dripping wet, not damp—which Randy pushed away, and we all returned to the room, where a silent group was fixated on watching our entry. Bless Mom—she always traveled with a first-aid kit. She took charge, shepherding Randy into the bathroom, where she ran cold water over the wound, applied a bit of antiseptic, and put a bandage over it—lots of moms travel with butterfly bandages, I guess. Then she made him take two aspirin, even over his objections.

"It doesn't hurt," he protested, but she answered darkly, "It will."

When Randy came out, he elaborated on what we'd heard on the phone. "This was preplanned," he said, "but I can't figure out the timing. How did they know when to pick her up? How did she know they'd be out there?"

We guessed everything from a prearranged time to a hidden phone on Adele—or maybe an Apple watch that would receive a coded message.

"It's a big deal in some ways, but what they didn't know is that we had a car in the parking lot, just in case of any kind of trouble. When they spotted the parked SUV with a man and woman in it, they just waited. Schmidt says they'll tail the car until it maybe leads them to Irene." He slammed his hand down on the table where he sat and then winced. "Nothing personal, but damn! I don't want to be here. I want to be in on the action."

# Chapter Sixteen

When there was a knock on the door, I thought for a panicky minute that the action had come to Randy, but then what was left of my rational mind reminded me about the officer seated outside the door. Still, I clutched Patrick's hand again—someone could have knocked the officer out.

Dad did the sensible thing—looked through the peephole and then opened the door. I nearly fainted when I saw Chance Charpentier standing there, still dressed in the suit and tie he'd had on at the signing. He had shed the jacket, his shirt was wrinkled, and the knot in his tie loosened and pulled well away from his throat. Last night he'd been dashing. This morning, he seemed to have aged overnight, with dark circles under his eyes and worry in them.

I thought about signaling Randy that the enemy had arrived, though I couldn't think of an inconspicuous way to do it. And in that moment, he didn't look like the enemy. Still, how did he get here? What had happened to our guard? Why didn't we hear anything? My horror increased when the guard appeared in the doorway, nodded at Chance, and pulled the door shut. Were they in collusion? The one good thought I clung to was that Chance obviously hadn't been in the car that picked up Adele.

"What . . . what are you doing here?"

Smooth as ever, he smiled. "I came to check on you, chérie. You were so distraught last night, and Detective Schmidt, he told me you spent the night on the couch in his waiting room. Uncomfortable, no?"

I nodded. "Uncomfortable, yes. You've talked to Schmidt this morning?" I began to fear the whole world was conspiring to botch up my wedding.

"Oui. And several times during the night." He shook his head. "I have not been able to find Irene, and I fear she is in the hands of crazy people. But I cleared up some other matters for Detective Schmidt. He said it was all right for me to come see you. I share your worry over Irene, though I am relieved that Mr. Peterman is safe and his injuries not more serious."

Patrick took over, I think because he sensed things were changing too fast for me to keep up. "Can you tell us what . . . ah . . . matters you cleared up for the detective?"

*Good! Patrick is as suspicious as I am.*

He shook his head. "I prefer that you hear that from an official. Meantime, I would be glad to buy everyone lunch. I understand you are advised not to leave the room, but I can have something brought in. A charcuterie, perhaps?"

Dad found his voice again. "That's kind of you, monsieur"—his pronunciation caused a slight wince from Chance— "but we just finished breakfast. I'm afraid we can't offer much in the way of accommodations, but won't you have a seat?" He gestured to the one easy chair in the room.

Chance sat, and once he was seated somehow the tension in the room lessened by maybe a tenth of one degree. We weren't relaxed, but he was now one of us. He cemented that by asking, "Do you mind if I keep vigil here with you? I don't think I could bear being alone in my hotel room." He seemed to be asking Dad and kept his eyes mostly fixed on him but with side glances toward me and Mom.

Dad ran a hand through his hair. "These are tough times for all of us. We would be glad to have you stay with us while we wait for word of Mrs. Foxglove."

It wasn't an easy morning. The girls dragged out a deck of cards and wheedled Randy into a game of Hearts, but none of them paid much attention to what they were doing and there was none of the hilarity that usually accompanied James' family games. I tried to get Chance to talk by asking questions, but his answers were monosyllabic.

I wasn't about to ask if he thought Irene was still alive—that would have been tempting fate—but I did ask why he thought the Parkers had kidnapped her. His answer was not what I expected at all.

"I think they are not very bright people," he said, speaking slowly as if choosing his words. "They think she still has the drugs, and they can force her to give them up. Then they can bargain to sell them to the people who transported them and killed the woman. If they run out of patience with Irene telling them she doesn't have the drugs...." His voice trailed off, and he shrugged. "Who knows?"

I shuddered. I didn't like the direction of his thoughts at all. "Aren't they playing a dangerous game?" I asked. "The people who originally smuggled the drugs might kill the Parkers." *And Adele!* Unbelievably, I felt protective about that brat of a child. I couldn't imagine that anyone would kill a child, but what Chance said was scary.

"Yes, that's true," Chance said calmly.

There it was—that thought again. Chance knew the Parkers might be killed, because he ordered it. *Stop that, Henny!* The man sitting in front of me wouldn't kill anyone, especially a child. All at once, I realized that was what I truly believed.

Randy broke in. "Sir, let's not scare everyone. We'll find her before anything bad happens."

Chance was gracious, if nothing else. "Of course. I am sorry if I misspoke. That was just my own thought, perhaps best kept to myself."

"Randy—" I got no further, because he interrupted me.

"Henny, there's a small army of police out there looking for her and for these Parker people. I expect any minute to hear that the Parkers led their tail right to her."

We lapsed into silence, as though, like Randy, we expected his mic to crackle to life momentarily. It didn't, and the silence stretched uncomfortably.

But Chance Charpentier had loosened his tongue, and he motioned for me to come sit by him. Since we had no chairs, I sat on the floor. Good thing because I might have fallen in another faint when he spoke.

His voice was soft. "I owe you a big debt that I've never yet had an opportunity to repay. Or even say thank you."

My expression surely told him I was puzzled.

"You saved Gabrielle, and probably Irene too, last year when a trusted employee of mine turned on me. Abel Dubois thought he would kidnap Gabrielle for a ransom. I was horrified when I found out I had trusted the wrong man. And at that, he hijacked my plane. It was good he was punished here, because I might have killed him if he appeared before me in France."

There it was, he talked casually of killing again. Did I believe this new story? I had no idea, but when he said, "You and Patrick must come to Aix-en-Provence and let me entertain you to show my gratitude," I wasn't quite ready to start packing my bags.

I murmured, "That's very kind of you. We . . . we cannot, any of us, plan anything until after the wedding."

Chance tried to make small talk, asking about Irene and her cooking show, and this time I was the one who was monosyllabic. I did manage to tell him that the show she taped would run next week.

"Ah, next week." He rubbed his chin with an open hand and said, "By next week, I hope she and I will both be back in France. I plan to leave the morning after your wedding."

My mind reeled—the wedding! The goal I'd been working toward all week. A hundred last-minute details jumped into my mind, not many of which I could do anything about. Should I call Claude and tell him to hold off on ordering fresh lobster—or tell him there might be extra mouths. What about flowers? I was just going to go to the florist this morning, Saturday, to choose from whatever they had—all I needed was two or three centerpieces. Probably Claude had a florist he could use, but would the flowers wilt unseen if the wedding was postponed? No, I wasn't going to think that way.

Mom's mind was running in the same track as mine, and she suddenly spoke up. "Randy, since we know now apparently that the Parkers have Irene and are trying to escape the police, can't we assume they won't go to Henny's apartment? I have food to prepare for tonight."

Randy shook his head. "Not until I get clearance. I'm sorry. I know you all would rather be planning for a wedding than sitting in this motel room."

Mom looked resigned, and I'm sure I was the picture of disappointment. Patrick muttered, "If we don't go to the Point tonight, I'll have spent five hundred bucks on Bluetooth portable speakers and now we'll never use them." I had no words for him. On our budget, that was a lot of money for something we'd use once, but he'd wanted so badly to play western music at the dinner. I couldn't even begin to think of a future where we might use Bluetooth speakers.

What seemed hours later but was really not quite noon, Randy's mic did come alive. As one, we tensed and listened as Schmidt said Irene was fine, on her way to Northwestern Memorial as a precaution. "We had a bit of trouble," he said, "but it's all done." He gave the all-clear for us to leave the hotel, though he added, "She wants to see Chance and Henny. Uh, it sounded like the lady is impatient."

We didn't focus on the bit of trouble. The words we heard were that she was alive and okay. Chance uttered a fervent "Merci!" and everyone began to talk. I didn't want to talk—I wanted to fly to the hospital.

Chance to the rescue. "My driver is waiting outside," he said to me. "Let us hurry."

I reached for Patrick's hand. I wasn't going without him. As we headed out the door, I threw Mom the key to my apartment and said, "I'll call as soon as we know something."

Irene was sitting on the edge of a gurney in an emergency room cubicle, dressed in a hospital gown, the look on her face murderous. Her first words to us were a demand, "Get me out of here! And I need some clothes. Henny, you'll have to go to the Palmer House and bring me some things. I will not wear that again." She gestured toward the lovely coral suit she'd worn last night, now crumpled and thrown on the floor.

I almost laughed, perhaps from relieved tension but more from the absurdity that she expected us to bust her out of an emergency room and me specifically to get her some clothes.

Before any of the three of us could speak, she had more to say. "Where is Raymond? That detective"—she gave the word an ominous twist as though it were distasteful—"said he's in this hospital. But it's as big as a city. I'll never find him. You must bring him to me."

I may not have felt capable right then of dealing with Irene's demands, but Chance was not intimidated. "Chérie, I will call Neiman Marcus and they will bring you something. I recommend a—what you call it?" He looked at me. "A sweat suit. You know, two pieces, pants and a jacket with a zipper? Gabrielle has such." Turning to Irene, he suggested, "You can talk to a sales assistant and have them bring two or three, so you can choose."

I suggested track suit might be the term, and he nodded. I wouldn't say Irene melted, but she began to defrost.

"I never . . . a track suit? Like young women wear when they pretend to exercise?"

Patrick hooted aloud, and I said, "Yes."

So it was done—a sales assistant would bring outfits as soon as possible. I wanted to hear what had happened to Irene—yes, I wanted all the grim details—but she would have nothing of it. With a wave of her hand, the diva was back.

She clutched her throat dramatically with one hand, while throwing the other arm in the air, and demanded, "Raymond! Where is Raymond? I must see that he is safe."

Chance, startled, jumped back to avoid the far-flung arm. "I believe you're right and he's in this hospital, chérie. But as to whether you can see him or not . . ." His voice trailed off, and he looked to me for rescue.

"This hospital is huge, Irene. We have no idea where he might be. All I can do is call the hospital operator and inquire."

She gave me a disdainful look, as though I were useless, and turned to Chance. "Can you not find a way to get me to him? He must be so worried."

Was she suggesting Chance bribe someone? Surely not. And when I thought she should be angry—terminally angry—at Ray Peterman, she was just the opposite.

John Wilson's arrival distracted all of us and put Irene in even more of a snit. "Irene," he said, bustling into the cubicle, which was getting pretty crowded, "I came as soon as I heard."

Repeating herself from earlier in the week, she said, "I have not done anything wrong. I do not need a lawyer." Gracious welcome, that!

"And thank goodness," John said. "Detective Schmidt kept me informed after you went missing, and he kindly called to tell me you were safe. I just want you to know I'm here for whatever I need."

The diva was disdainful. "I need nothing. Except Raymond."

That confused John, but before I could explain, Chance stepped forward. "Monsieur, I am Chance Charpentier, an old friend of Irene's from France."

That, I thought, was a neat way of telescoping the truth.

"And I am grateful to you for any help you have given her. Perhaps you have a card you could give me. I expect to be with Irene until she returns to France."

Did anyone hear that great sigh of relief I inadvertently released. Patrick did, and his eyes smiled at me.

John Wilson dug into his ever-present briefcase and extracted a business card. Then belatedly, he realized he had not shaken hands with Chance, so there followed an awkward moment in which he tried to simultaneously shake hands and transfer the card. That done, he was like a deflated balloon. "If there's nothing further, I'll just be on my way and trust you to call me if needed, monsieur." He butchered that last word.

"Let's walk out with Mr. Wilson," Patrick said. "Maybe we can talk to a nurse."

Did he think ER nurses were just standing around, with nothing to do but talk to him? Why wasn't Irene telling us what happened? Didn't she realize we had been worried—make that terrified—for her? And I was angry at her for being so rude to John Wilson. My anger at the victim made me stomp out of the cubicle.

Wilson, however, was not bothered. "I see that France has not changed Irene," he said with a chuckle. "Good luck with your wedding. And with our favorite chef." And he was gone, scurrying down the hall.

"Patrick," I whispered, "unless we walk away, Irene and Chance will hear everything we say."

Patrick was ahead of me, as usual. With a finger to his lips indicating silence, he pulled me toward the waiting room. Once there, he practically forced me to sit in one of the hard plastic chairs. I'd had enough of plastic furniture, thank you.

"Henny, let her have her moment. She's playing Chance off against Ray, and I doubt she realizes Ray may face criminal charges for his part in this, even if he cooperated with those people under threats. Don't get in her way now."

I wanted to cry . . . and I did. "But it's our wedding. After all this, she's still going to ruin it."

"You know what will ruin it? You and me, if we're grumpy tonight or tomorrow. We're going to check with the nurse and find out Irene's status, and then we're going to leave Chance with her and go take a good nap."

A nap. Yes! I was exhausted. Drying my tears—honest, they were not crocodile tears—I stood up and put my arms around him. "I love you," was all I said, and I probably didn't even need to say it aloud.

That's just what we did. We stopped the first nurse we saw, a man who I mistook for an orderly, which caused Patrick to pinch me, a reminder that not all nurses are female. This man happened to have been assigned to Irene (along with too many other patients) and was honest with us. "Your friend is overwrought," he said. "Her vitals are sort of off the chart . . ."

Could I tell him she probably lived that way?

"The doctor has written an order for sedation and is keeping her overnight."

"She will not be happy," I warned.

His smile was tired. "Most patients aren't."

Chance was agreeable to our plan and announced that once Irene was in a room, he would doze in a chair. I didn't tell him it could be hours before she was in a room.

Patrick called for an Uber because his car was at the police station. We'd Uber over to get it and then go home. While we waited, he said, "Great idea to leave them. I think Chance wanted time to be alone with her."

"My ideas about him have done a complete turn since he arrived. I was so sure he was the villain behind all this trouble. Now I think he's her best chance. I hope she goes back to France on that plane with him."

Mom was at the apartment, fiddling with the dinner, packing up picnic gear—I had decreed no disposable plates because we didn't want to create that much trash, so she was packing the family tinware, that speckled blue stuff I had loved since childhood.

We hugged her and announced we were going to Patrick's apartment to nap. She didn't bat an eye at the impropriety of it all, and I was almost too tired to care, although at the same time I was sure I had too much on my mind to sleep. Silly me. I slept hard for three hours and woke groggy to find Patrick, freshly changed into clean clothes, in the kitchen with Mom. The family, they told me, were waiting at the Point.

# Chapter Seventeen

If you happened to wander out to Chicago's Promontory Point that warm June night, you'd have thought we were having the jolliest party ever. And in many ways, we were. The rich smell of barbecue crowded out the freshness of the lake when Dad fired up one of the public grills to reheat the meat. Mom dished out potato salad and coleslaw, and everyone ate almost all of the two briskets Dad had done, most of the potato salad and slaw. The pinto beans were perfect, and Patrick demanded to know why I'd never fixed them for him. He'd never tasted beans like that. Wasn't worth explaining that a pot of beans for two people might last to eternity, and I wasn't serving canned beans. I remembered that TV segment about Texas barbecue that Bob said we'd do after our honeymoon. I'd add beans to the menu and share with the studio crew.

After everyone had eaten too much, we danced off the excess pounds. Patrick had loaded the Bose system with the music I listed, and in the dusk the strains of "Cotton Eyed Joe," "Amarillo By Morning," and "Take Me Home, Country Roads" drifted out over the lake as my sisters taught Chance Charpentier how to do the Cotton Eyed Joe and to do fancier two-step moves. He was a quick take and seemed to love it, throwing back his head in laughter. Al Schmidt refused the girls' offer of a lesson but sat watching and clapping his hands rhythmically to the music. Mom and Dad, having danced together for long years, glided around the spacious pavilion, putting everyone else in the shade.

The evening ended with another James' family tradition. We had a singalong, visiting all the old favorites—"Kumbaya," "Michael, Row the Boat Ashore," "On Top of Old Smoky," "John Jacob Jingleheimer Schmidt," even those childhood favorites, "Do Your Ears Hang Low?" and "Wheels on the Bus." It was definitely a James' family affair as we tried to urge everyone else to join in. Clearly most of them didn't know the lyrics, and I wondered about their childhoods. For me, it was a sentimental moment, as though I were bidding my own childhood farewell. Chance broke that mood by leading us in "Frère Jacques" and then the more gentle, "Au Clair De La Lune."

But the be-still-my-heart moment came when Patrick proposed a toast to me and asked that we all sing "Stand By Me." A rousing end to the evening.

Only appearances are deceiving. None of us were as jolly as we were pretending. Too many tensions and unresolved questions lay just beneath the surface of our good times. We missed those who weren't with us—principally Irene and Ray Peterman. Randy Collins had begged off, saying his girlfriend would kill him if he went to a party after the week they'd had—or not had, and Linda Rutledge was recovering after her scare. But the unexpected arrival of both Chance and Al Schmidt, trailed by Skylar Calhoun, was a welcome surprise, although I thought it the most unlikely threesome I'd ever seen. Why did Al Schmidt and Chance come together and act, well, almost chummy? And what was Skylar doing with them? True, Schmidt was her boss and Patrick had invited her, but still. She was much less in command than she had been in my apartment and looked a lot more tentative, unsure. And Chance—how had he escaped Irene's clutches? What was the medical report on Ray Peterman?

Patrick's parents were a puzzle—a difficult one and for me, not a happy one. Patrick had to go to the Sophy to pick them up, and they were appalled to find that they couldn't drive right up to the shelter but had to walk a city block or more from the viaduct where the Outer Drive went over the path to the Point. They were dressed for neither walking nor a barbecue—Joanna wore tan cotton pants, perfectly fitted, a silk shirt, and a summer-weight matching sweater thrown over her shoulders, plus of course a chunky necklace that looked like amber. And on her feet? Tan heels that were too high for comfort. Reid O'Malley was in a blue blazer with the brass nautical buttons, seersucker pants, and a white Polo shirt—he looked more ready for a day on a yacht than a barbecue.

Once there, they had greeted me with half-hearted handshakes and emotionless words about how relieved they were that "things worked out," as though they were referring to a big secret no one else understood. They picked at their food and looked grim during the dancing, their expressions clearly saying they were waiting out the time until they could escape to their posh hotel. Of course, there was no way Joanna could have done the Cotton Eyed Joe in those shoes.

My mom watched them with close attention and began to plan her own behavior in reaction. At one point, she threw her arms around a startled Patrick and cried, "I can't wait to have a son in the family." He hugged her back and announced that he too was anxious to be part of the family. Another time, Mom clapped her hands to get everyone's attention and demanded a round of cheers for "the pitmaster, who makes the best brisket in all of Texas. If you liked our barbecue tonight, give him a big hand."

Later, as Patrick was about to walk his parents back to their car, his mother gushed too obviously, "I can't believe Patrick hasn't brought you to Winnetka. You must come visit, and we'll give you some good northern food, like sweet beans."

I managed a polite smile and bit my tongue to keep from calling her Mrs. O'Malley. After all, she hadn't invited me to call her Joanna. Or he, Reid. Their parting words were stiff: "We look forward to the wedding tomorrow." Sure they did!

I told myself I loved Patrick enough to deal with these cold people, and it would all work out with time. Whether or not I believed that is another thing, but there was no way they would make me hesitate over the wedding I'd fought so hard for.

Much more troubling were the questions that bounced around in my head even as I ate and danced and sang: Why were Schmidt and Chance Charpentier now such good friends? Why had the Parkers kidnapped Irene? What had happened to them—and to Adele? What had Chance meant when he said he took care of some other matters for Al Schmidt? Who killed Simone Guillaume and why? Who was running drugs and what happened to them? Until I knew all that, I would never feel that Irene was truly safe—or that my wedding would go as planned.

When I tried to approach Schmidt with some of these questions, he was busy whispering something to Skylar. She had been a spectator to the evening—eating but declining to sing or dance, and yet somehow, I sensed she enjoyed herself—as much as she ever did. Schmidt, being almost fatherly toward his charge, brushed me away with a wave of the hand and "Later. Not now." Okay, a barbecue/rehearsal dinner was admittedly neither the time nor place, but what was?

As he left, Schmidt pulled me aside. "Breakfast at nine at the Starbucks on Fifty-Fifth? Just you. Not this whole gang." He nodded his head toward my family, who were clustered over the tables, cleaning up.

My first thought was, "I am getting married tomorrow evening. I can't do this." But I quickly realized I could and would because I had to have this all settled once and for all. But I had one stipulation: "Patrick comes with me."

Schmidt shrugged and gave me a light, friendly hug. "See you there. Don't be late."

*As if!*

Schmidt was not yet there when Patrick and I arrived. I ordered a cinnamon dolce latte and a cheddar, sausage, and egg breakfast sandwich. He frowned at me, muttered "too many flavors too early in the morning," and ordered dark roast misto and a plain croissant. We munched in silence and waited impatiently.

When Schmidt arrived, to my dismay he was not alone. Chance Charpentier strode in behind him, impeccably dressed in a gray suit, white shirt, and red patterned tie, a sharp contrast to Schmidt's too-baggy pants and rumpled shirt. Chance looked like he'd gotten a good night's sleep; Schmidt did not.

At least Skylar's not with them, I thought.

They ordered coffee, no food, and sat down with us. No preliminaries, no polite chitchat. "Chance has a confession to make," Schmidt said.

I nearly fell off my chair. Even Patrick's steadying hand on my thigh was no guarantee I wouldn't just slide down on the floor. I waited, my imagination half expecting Schmidt to call in some officers to slap handcuffs on Chance. *Stop it, Henny!*

Chance began a long way before Irene's kidnapping. "My father," he said, "was a happily married man and a doting parent to me, but his wife, my mother, died early, and he was alone with me."

*Where was this going? What could it possibly have to do with what happened to Irene?*

"But he was, like many men of means in my country"—he paused, cleared his throat, and went on—"a man who enjoyed women. Beautiful women. He was particularly fond of a certain madam in Paris. Because he frequented her residence, he knew all her, ah, employees. And as I was growing up, he often took me there." He hesitated, then quickly added, "He put me in the kitchen with the cook while he did whatever he did." Chance didn't seem to want to explore that but instead added, "That's why I am a good cook today."

Even Schmidt was getting impatient, drumming his fingers on the table. My sandwich sat cooling, untouched since they sat down, though I noticed Patrick had finished his croissant.

"I have remained in touch with that madam, principally because I administer the trust my father left to her. I became aware in, oh, the last year perhaps, that something was, how you say it? Fishy? One or the other of the girls would take sudden, quick trips to the States, returning within days. Simone Guillaume was one of those girls. The trip on which she died was not her first."

"She was a courier," Schmidt said bluntly. "Carrying drugs from France to the U.S. for a group of smugglers. She delivered them to a network here in Chicago." He was determined to shorten what was looking like a long story.

"So why did she put the drugs in Irene's bag instead of delivering them?" It seemed to me a logical question. "And why did Irene claim she didn't know her?"

He chuckled. "Irene would never admit to knowing a lady of the night." He paused thoughtfully. "For several months, I did not know Simone was in Aix-en-Peyrolles. When I found out, I was angry, because I thought she went there to cultivate Irene."

I was horrified. It all seemed part of a much larger, darker scheme than I had imagined.

Chance shrugged. "Simone is dead. We may never know for certain why she did what she did, but I suspect she had displeased someone here, and she feared for her life. Perhaps she would seek protection and reveal the smugglers, but she couldn't do it with the drugs on her person."

It was Patrick's turn to guess. "But whoever she was to deliver them to found out she had double-crossed them and killed her? Wow!"

Schmidt said, "Yeah, wow. When Chance here mentioned he had connections in Chicago, I saw an opportunity to unravel a drug problem we've been chasing for a couple of years and solve a murder at the same time."

"Business connections," Chance said with emphasis. "I have never actually been to Chicago before. I hope to see more of the charming city."

Schmidt brushed that aside, with a wave of his hand. "He spent Friday night tracing that network. By Saturday morning, we had three primary suspects in custody. Great work on his part."

"But you didn't find Irene," I protested.

"Didn't expect to. I had a whole army working on finding her, but I knew the smugglers were too smart to think she still had the drugs. Whoever took her had to be an amateur."

"The Parkers," I said, letting out a huge breath.

"Yes, the Parkers," Chance said. "They were planning to use the drugs they thought Irene still had to bargain with the smugglers. Thought they would make a lot of money easily. But, what is it you told them?" He turned to Schmidt.

"There ain't no free lunch, even in the criminal world," the police officer said gruffly.

Chance elaborated. "Mrs. Parker confessed while in jail, because she was concerned about her child."

I thought Emily Parker should have thought of that before she let herself be part of the harebrained scheme. "Adele?"

"With Child Protective Services. There's a grandmother who's on her way from California to get her." Schmidt's voice lowered. "North Parker is in critical care at Cook County, under guard. We're not sure he'll make it."

"Make it? As in he might die?" Despite the death of two women over these drugs, Parker's condition made things a lot worse. Maybe it was how close Irene had come to death. "What happened?"

"He tried to shoot a police office. It was a dumb thing to do." Schmidt was matter-of-fact about it.

I sat for a long minute, trying to piece all this together in my mind. There was one tiny piece left unsettled. "Ray Peterman? Will he be charged?"

As Chance shook his head and murmured, "So sad," Schmidt said, "He's not recovering like the docs want. They say he'll never be able to work again, and he may need daily assistance, like a home. Blows to the head can really do a number on older folks." After a second, he added, "There won't be any charges."

"The worst of it is that there was no one in Peoria to threaten his sister. The Parkers made that up." Chance shrugged again. "I should rejoice. My rival for Irene's affection is now out of the picture. But I am sad for the man. He was good to her, and I like him."

I felt like weeping for all the trouble—and death—that greed had caused. First the smugglers, then the Parkers. And I guess we couldn't overlook Simone—she must have done what she did for money, until she got scared. The innocent victims were Irene, Ray Peterman, and Janis Simmons, the English woman killed in France.

"It really is all over?" I asked.

Schmidt nodded, but Chance was on his feet. "I must go to the hospital. Your Ms. Rutledge is with Irene, but she will be dismissed shortly, and I will undertake to see that she rests so that she can be bright at the wedding tonight."

I turned to Schmidt. "You'll come to the wedding?"

He shook his head. "I'm going home and will sleep for four days."

To my pleased delight, Ray Peterman was at our wedding after all. Chance Charpentier had arranged for a car and driver to pick up Ray and his niece, Betty, at the hospital, and Betty pushed her uncle around in a wheelchair. He looked frail but although I was prepared for confusion on his part, he seemed to know everyone and be glad to be with us. Irene fluttered over him like a mother hen, adjusting his lap blanket, even smoothing his hair. Chance watched with a bemused expression.

Glad as we were to see Peterman, Patrick and I didn't spend much time watching him. We had something much more important on our minds. Patrick had asked a faculty member of the theology department at his university to perform the brief ceremony. We both opted for the traditional words—no, we didn't write our own vows, except to take out the obedience clause—and there was no music. The Palmer House did not play Muzak for its guests, and I was grateful. After all, one of our goals was to draw as little attention as possible to a wedding in the grand lobby of the hotel. We didn't want other guests either disturbed or gawking at us. Jim Holcomb was on hand—just to be sure all went well, he told us, though I suspected he was also there in support of Betty and Ray Peterman.

Ten people stood quietly for the ceremony, murmuring their congratulations instead of the traditional clapping. My dress was what I wanted, barring that little pucker at the waist where the alteration had not quite worked. I never did get to try it on, but I blessed Patrick for rushing Sunday afternoon to Mrs. Adams' house to pick it up. Patrick—what can I say about Patrick except that he looked wonderful. He had surprised me with a two-piece suit. No, not a traditional one—this was gray pants and a matching vest, over a medium blue shirt that made his eyes shine. Hmm, maybe that wasn't all that made his eyes shine. When the minister pronounced us man and wife, we kissed, and I took a long look heavenward—no one would ever know if I was looking at that magnificent, frescoed ceiling or talking to the Lord.

Joanna O'Malley was true to form at the reception. Her third glass of wine in hand before we even got to the appetizers, she said, "Such a lovely simple ceremony. Of course, we had wished a large church wedding for Patrick, but at this point we're just glad he's married." The implication I heard was better marry an unsatisfactory bride than none at all. But then she turned to me and said, "Well, now you are Mrs. Patrick O'Malley."

"No. I'm still Henrietta James, better known as Henny. That's who Patrick married."

But the O'Malleys' stiffness was barely noticed by most of the guests. Irene apparently forgot that the guests were assembled to see us wed and assumed instead that they had come to hear the details of her recent "ordeal."

"I can't tell you," she proclaimed to several gathered around her, "how devastated I felt when I was handcuffed to that bed."

I did almost gasp. I had wanted to know about the kidnapping, but I didn't want such grisly details at my wedding.

Irene was not to be deterred. "And when they bashed poor Raymond in the head, I was terrified. For him, of course. I knew that I would survive." She went on with descriptions of being blindfolded and driven here and there, her hunger because no one had fed her, and other details I was quite sure she should have omitted.

Patrick and I stood to one side, holding hands and watching the scene. Raymond looked down at his lap, as though ashamed of his part in what had happened, and Chance watched with that same amused look on his face. My sisters were enthralled, and even Joanna and Reid lost their bored expressions. My parents looked displeased, but only to me because I knew them well.

At one point, Chance came over and stood with us while we watched Irene's performance—there was no other word for it. Surprising me, in a soft voice, he said, "I should have married her. I knew it the minute she left France, but I was too damn young and stubborn." Without another word, he moved away from us.

Everyone was enjoying the appetizers, and no one missed the pâté and gougères Irene hadn't had time to make, just as no one mentioned the bridal luncheon that never happened. Patrick eventually said, "Henny, our guests are getting hungry, and my mother is drinking too much wine. I'm afraid she'll start telling people she wanted me to marry Maddie."

"We should have invited her to the wedding," I said and meant it. Still, I was surprised when he said, "I did. But she and her new fiancé are in New York this weekend."

I stared at him. "I suppose you invited Skylar too."

Not at all embarrassed, he said, "I did. But she was too shy. I told her we'd take her to dinner next week."

*While we're on our honeymoon!* Skylar Calhoun was going to be part of my life, but it was okay. I had Patrick, and that's what mattered.

Prompted by Patrick's fear of what his mother would say next, I asked Claude to serve the dinner, while Patrick went from person to person urging each to find his or her place at the three tables. I had laboriously hand-lettered place cards and then hastily at the last minute added them for Chance, Betty, and Ray Peterman.

Claude outdid himself. The lobster thermidor was superb, and I vowed to make it for Patrick sometime to see if I could equal Claude's skill. Ellie poked at it, until Mom frowned at her, and I heard her whisper, "Well, I would have eaten a hamburger."

We cut the chocolate mousse cake we had chosen amid a shower of good wishes and cake-cutting advice, but we forswore the tradition of feeding each other. I'd seen too many brides and grooms smear cake all over each other's faces.

All in all, it was the quiet, sophisticated but low-key wedding I had wanted all along, and I was pleased. I finally believed it would really happen, and Irene hadn't ruined it at all—except for monopolizing attention before dinner. She made up for that with a graceful toast. When Chance raised his glass and said, "To the bride and groom," she held up a hand. With almost a quaver in her voice, Irene said, "I hope Cindy and Gene will forgive me"—the first time she'd used my parents' given names—"but I feel that Henrietta is part my daughter too. I've taught her as best I could the intricacies of French cooking"—Patrick squeezed my hand, a signal to keep my mouth shut—"and she has helped me, guided me, and yes, rescued me, more times than I can count. And now she is marrying this wonderful young man, Patrick. *Bons voeux de bonheur mariage.*" She raised her glass dramatically and took a long swallow.

Everyone began to drift away—Chance to take Irene to her hotel room, Betty to take Ray back to the hospital, the O'Malleys for the drive to Winnetka—they couldn't wait to get back to their own comfort zone. My family were the last to leave and did with many hugs and not a few tears. We would not see them for months, since they would leave for Texas in the morning, but we promised to spend Christmas in Fort Worth.

And then Patrick and I went on our honeymoon—three floors up to a smaller suite in the Palmer House for one elegant night.

We were married. I let out a long sigh of relief.

# Epilogue

Tuesday morning and two days married, Patrick and I made that long drive west on Fifty-Fifth Street to Midway Airport—Chicago had plenty of freeways, but they mostly went north and south, so I saw up close the busy commercial area I was used to and then residential neighborhoods in various states of repair, all a part of the city I'd made my home and yet didn't know well.

Chance's private plane had flown into Midway, rather than the bigger and busier O'Hare, mostly because Midway was so much closer to Hyde Park. The pilot and one attendant had been on call, in a hotel, waiting for Chance to signal the flight back to Aix-en-Provence. They were scheduled to leave at ten in the morning.

Irene's leave-taking was even more dramatic than her arrival had been nine days earlier—I couldn't believe it had only been nine days. She hugged us and kissed our cheeks and thanked us at least ten times for getting her out of danger and for coming to the airport. Chance assured us the plane was fully stocked with everything from food and wine to tranquilizers and medical supplies for the thirteen-hour flight. I pushed away thoughts of thirteen being unlucky and thanked him. And when he again invited us to France, I told him it was on our bucket list. It was his turn to be curious. "Bucket list?"

Curiosity overwhelmed me, and I accepted too quickly when we were invited aboard. Wood paneling, soft leather couches in a warm beige tone with contrasting throw pillows, a table set for an intimate meal for two, with linen napkins and crystal wine glasses. A small galley apparently could produce gourmet meals, and the restroom was twice the size of those cramped quarters on commercial airlines.

Irene gave us one last hug and sank onto one of the couches, apparently exhausted. I hugged Chance tightly, my way of apologizing, and he and Patrick even hugged. Then, within seconds, we were back inside the airport, tourists watching the plane take off.

As it rose, banked, and turned, Patrick was the one who murmured, "Au revoir, Irene."

And I replied, "Don't worry. She'll be back."

## *From Irene's French Kitchen*

**Lobster Thermidor**

    Irene and Claude, the Palmer House chef, would both insist on using live lobster for this dish, but Henny is pragmatic. She knew that trying to boil live lobsters on a TV set with Irene "helping" would lead to disaster. She opted for lobster tails. If you want to be a purist and spend a day on the dish, including probably buying a bigger pot to boil the lobster, Henny refers you to Julia Child's recipe online.

    Here's what Henny did:

4 *(6- to 8-ounce)* lobster tails *(be sure they are large enough to stuff)*

4 tablespoons butter, divided

1 small white onion, finely chopped

2 tbsp. flour

Glug of white wine

½ c. milk

½ c. sharp cheddar, white cheddar preferred

½ tsp. Old Bay seafood seasoning

2 tbsp. grated Parmesan or Pecorino

2 tbsp. breadcrumbs

    Boil lobster tails 7 to 8 minutes, until shell turns bright red. Drain and immediately submerge in cold ice water to stop the cooking. With your kitchen scissors, cut the soft underside of the tails down the middle. Remove meat and put the empty shells in a shallow casserole dish. Chop the cooked meat into bite-sized pieces.

    In a small pot, melt 2 tbsp. butter over medium heat. Sauté the chopped onion until soft. Add the flour, stir to make a paste, and cook another two or three minutes. Stir in wine, followed by milk. Take the pan off the stove and stir in cheddar cheese and seafood seasoning. Add salt and pepper to taste. Add lobster meat to the sauce and stir to combine.

Spoon mixture into shells, mounding for a generous presentation. Top with grated cheese and breadcrumbs.

Broil on high until golden, 2 or 3 minutes. Plate on a bed of greens and garnish with lemon slices or wedges.

**Gougères**

Gougères are small appetizers made of a rich dough called choux pastry and cheese, traditionally Comté, Emmentaler, or Gruyère. The ingredients are simple, but making the pastries involves a lot of beating by hand.

6 tbsp. unsalted butter, cut into small pieces

¾ tsp. salt, preferably kosher

Pinch of nutmeg

1 c. water

1-1/4 c. flour

4 eggs

1-1/2 c. Comté, Emmentaler, or Gruyère cheese, grated

½ tsp. fine black pepper

One egg yolk

Combine first four ingredients in a saucepan and bring to a boil. Cook, just below a boil, until butter is melted. Stir in the flour. Cook over medium heat, stirring constantly, until mixture forms a ball in the middle of the pan. Dough should not be sticky. Let it cool slightly, because you will be adding eggs but don't want the dough to cook them before you can stir them in.

When the dough has cooled, beat the eggs in one at a time, beating vigorously after each egg until it is thoroughly incorporated into the dough. Do not try to hurry the process by adding all four eggs at once. After the last egg, stir in cheese and pepper.

Line a baking sheet with parchment paper. Irene shapes the dough into one-inch balls by hand, but Henny prefers to use a piping bag with the ½" round tip. You may also cut the corner off a plastic bag and use it as a homemade piping bag. Place dough balls 2" apart on baking sheet as they will expand.

Make an egg wash with remaining egg yolk and 1 tsp. water. Brush onto gougères before baking.

Bake at 400° for 20-25 minutes. When done, they will be golden brown. You can test for doneness by breaking one open: it should be dry on the inside.

Recipe makes about 50 gougères, but people will eat several at a time.

## Gibelotte

A gibelotte is a French stew of either fish or rabbit. Henny can find rabbit at specialty markets in Chicago, but she has been hesitant to try that on Patrick and certainly wouldn't alienate the viewers of her TV show by serving the Easter bunny. For American tastes, you could substitute chicken, although Madame would dismiss it as unworthy. Veal, although expensive, would be another choice. This is a basic recipe; if you wish you may add sliced mushrooms, or baby carrots, or tiny new potatoes.

4 lbs. meat of your choice, in serving size pieces

Four strips bacon

2 tbsp. flour

2 c. chicken broth, prepared or made from condensed base

2 c. dry white wine

1 bouquet garni*

2 tbsp. tomato paste

Salt and pepper to taste

¼ c. heavy cream

Toss the meat pieces in flour, salt, and pepper.

Fry the bacon until the grease is rendered *(if you keep bacon fat in the refrigerator, as Irene does, you may use that)*. Remove bacon and brown meat in fat.

Add remaining ingredients except the cream. Simmer the gibelotte over low heat until meat is tender and thoroughly cooked, usually about an hour and a half. You may also bake at 325°.

Remove meat to a platter and tent to keep warm; remove bouquet garni from the sauce and strain the sauce. Add cream. Transfer to a saucepan and heat until slightly thickened. Pour sauce over meat and serve.

*Bouquet garni: use kitchen string to tie together a spring of Italian parsley, a bay leaf, and two sprigs of thyme. Or use a tsp. each of thyme and parsley and a bay leaf.

**Salade Niçoise**

Salade Niçoise is built around tuna—in France, undoubtedly fresh tuna, but a high-quality, canned variety is perfectly acceptable. Henny likes to do it with canned albacore in olive oil.

Olives, green or ripe, are traditional, but Henny omits them because olives are on the short list of things she just doesn't eat, along with bell peppers. If you like them, you may want to add strips, preferably of red peppers. Anchovies are a truly French contribution to the salad, and if you like them, they add a wonderful zing. Julia Child added an anchovy filet, twisted, on each hard-boiled egg quarter and scattered capers and chopped parsley on the finished salad.

The thing about this main-dish salad is you can create it to your taste. Choose the vegetables you prefer, but with an eye to color and appearance. Suggestions include tiny baby potatoes, peeled, boiled, and cut in quarters, if necessary, haricort vert (those tiny French green beans), artichoke hearts quartered, cherry tomatoes, hard-boiled eggs. Sometimes Henny adds tender, young asparagus spears if in season. She believes in simplicity—too many vegetables spoil the presentation.

Pour a little dressing over the potatoes when they are warm—they'll absorb it better. Each vegetable and the tuna should be seasoned with a little dressing before becoming part of the arrangement. Lay out the vegetables and tuna in an attractive pattern, either on a platter or individual plates, on a bed of lettuce. Some cooks group ingredients; others prefer a more casual arrangement. Pour any remaining dressing over. If you need another batch of dressing, by all means make it. You don't want soup, but you don't want a dry salad.

Vinaigrette is the traditional dressing for Salade Niçoise. Here's the one Henny frequently uses (enough for two individual salads):

¼ c. olive oil

2 tbsp. red wine vinegar

2 tbsp. lemon juice

1 clove garlic, pressed

1 tsp. Dijon mustard

½ tsp. salt

¼ tsp. pepper

## And from Henny's Mom's Texas Kitchen
### Henny's Mom's Ranch Beans

1 lb. dry pinto beans

1 large white onion, chopped

¼ lb. salt pork or fat back, diced

5 beef bouillon cubes or 5 tsp. condensed base

Rinse and sort a pound of uncooked pinto beans, discarding any that are broken or wrinkled. In a Dutch oven, cover beans with cold water an inch above the level of the beans. Soak overnight.

Next morning, drain the beans and cover with fresh water. Sauté salt pork until fat is rendered. Add chopped onion and sauté until translucent. Dump onion and fat into beans. Bring to just beneath a boil, lower heat, and simmer. Do not let the beans boil—there are lots of old wives' tales about the bad things that happen if you do, particularly to your digestive system, and just as many remedies for the problem, but it's best to just be sure they simmer all day. About twenty minutes before serving, stir in beef bouillon cubes or condensed base. Increase heat just a little to make sure bouillon is incorporated throughout. Serve with Texas toast, cornbread, or tortillas to mop up the "pot likker."

### Henny's Mom's Potato Salad

> 3 lbs. potatoes, boiled, peeled, and diced
>
> Vinaigrette *(optional)*
>
> ½ c. sweet onion, diced
>
> 4 hard-boiled eggs, diced
>
> 2 tbsp. dill pickle juice
>
> ½ c. dill pickle relish
>
> 2 c. mayo
>
> ¼ c. Dijon mustard
>
> ¼ tsp. pepper
>
> 2-1/2 tsp. salt
>
> Dash of paprika

There are two schools of thought about potato salad. Henny's mom dices the hot potatoes and tosses with just a bit of vinaigrette dressing. She believes the warm potatoes absorb the vinaigrette better. Then she lets them sit until cool enough to handle, and meanwhile she makes the dressing. Henny finds it a pain to peel hot potatoes. She boils the unpeeled potatoes, refrigerates until chilled, and then finds them easier to peel and dice.

Either way, at that point, you mix it all together. Both Henny and her mom, though, recommend mixing the dressing ingredients separately and then pouring over potatoes. Do not add ingredients one at a time to the potatoes—the dressing will never evenly incorporate all ingredients if you do that.

# About Judy Alter

After an award-winning career writing historical fiction about women of the nineteenth-century American West, Judy Alter turned her attention to contemporary cozy mysteries. She is the author of three series: Kelly O'Connell Mysteries, Blue Plate Café Mysteries, and Oak Grove Mysteries. *Irene in Danger* is the second in her Irene in Chicago Culinary Mysteries. Find Judy and a list of her books at http://www.judyalter.com.

Judy is an active member of Sisters in Crime, Guppies, Story Circle Network, Women Writing the West, and the Texas Institute of Letters. When she is not writing, she is busy with seven grandchildren and a lively poodle/border collie cross. Her avocation is cooking, and she is the author of *Cooking My Way Through Life with Kids and Books, Gourmet on a Hot Plate,* and *Texas is Chili Country.*

Born in Chicago, she has made her home in Fort Worth for over fifty years.

Did you enjoy Irene's latest adventure?
If so, please write a brief review
Goodreads: https://www.goodreads.com, or
Amazon: https://www.amazon.com/books
And be sure to watch for
*Irene Keeps a Secret*
Coming soon

Made in the USA
Coppell, TX
04 November 2021